Praise for Donald Barthelme

"A pacifist tract, a rueful travesty, a bumptious 'feast of blague,' and a dazzlement of style both minimal and musical."
—*New Yorker*

"An absolute charmer, funny, sexy, and serene. . . . Every page sparkles in *The King*."
—Michael Dirda, *Washington Post*

"All hail to *The King*."
—Herbert Mitgang, *New York Times*

"The king is noble, the comedy autumnal, and the style is glorious indeed."
—Richard Locke, *Wall Street Journal*

"*The King* is quintessential Barthelme, a laboratory in which forms of shopworn discourse are examined and exposed. The parodic impulse is wildly unreined."
—Jay Parini, *New York Times Book Review*

"Vaudeville deflates chivalry, while the conflict between medieval belief and modern presumption is gift-wrapped in a fluent mixture of lyrical turns and metafictional badinage."
—*America*

Other Books by Donald Barthelme

Donald Barthelme

The King

Illustrations by Barry Moser

DALKEY ARCHIVE PRESS
NORMAL · LONDON

First published by HarperCollins, 1990
Copyright © 1990 by The Estate of Donald Barthelme
Wood engravings copyright © 1990 by Pennyroyal Press, Inc.

First Dalkey Archive edition, 2006
All rights reserved

Library of Congress Cataloging-in-Publication Data available.
ISBN: 1-56478-413-4

Partially funded by a grant from the Illinois Arts Council, a state agency.

Dalkey Archive Press is a nonprofit organization whose mission is
to promote international cultural understanding and provide
a forum for dialogue for the literary arts.

www.dalkeyarchive.com

Printed on permanent/durable acid-free paper, bound in the
United States of America, and distributed throughout
North America and Europe.

To Anne and Katharine

THE
KING

"EE THERE! It's Launcelot!"

"Riding, riding—"

"How swiftly he goes!"

"As if enchafed by a fiend!"

"The splendid muscles of his horse move rhythmically under the drenchèd skin of same!"

"By Jesu, he is in a vast hurry!"

"But now he pulls up the horse and sits for a moment, lost in thought!"

"Now he wags his great head in daffish fashion!"

"He reins the horse about and puts the golden spurs to her!"

"But that is the direction from which he lately came with such excess of speed!"

"No, it's slightly different! It's at an angle of about fifteen degrees to the first!"

"This breakbone pace will soon unhorse him!"

I

"Not Launcelot! Launcelot is the greatest horseman in the realm!"

"Look you! Launcelot and his horse have plunged into a deep mire!"

"He's thrown! The horse is down!"

"Now the horse struggles to his feet! But Launcelot's still on the ground! Perhaps he's broken something!"

"No, he's up, he inspects the horse, he leaps into the saddle, he reins about once again— Now he rides off furiously in still another way!"

"He burns the ground in his careening!"

"It is as if he hears beams a-bugling from every quarter of the compass!"

"His responsibilities are grave and many!"

"Look there, there is another knight in Launcelot's path the twain have fewtered their spears they hurtle fast together the knight who is not Sir Launcelot is shocked out of the saddle he rises in the air turning end over end—"

"Launcelot wallops on doesn't even stop to smite the fellow's head off but pounds ever more fiercely toward a distant goal—"

"I'm losing sight of him, his figure dwindles and grows small!"

"I can see him still, getting smaller and smaller in the remote distance!"

"Riding, riding—"

UINEVERE in London, at the palace. Sitting in a chair buttering an apple.

"I am getting sick, sore, and tired of this," she said.

"Yes, mum," said Varley.

"Good evening, fellow Englishmen," the radio said. "This is Germany calling."

"A fundamentally disagreeable voice," said Guinevere, "stale cabbage."

"The invincible forces of the Reich," said Haw-Haw, "are advancing on all fronts. Dunkirk has been completely secured. The slaughter is very great. Gawain has been reported captured—"

"Not in a hundred million years," said Guinevere. "Gawain will pepper their pork for them."

"The false and miscreant king, Arthur, languishes meanwhile at Dover, according to my spies. Conspicuously alone. No Guinevere. I think we may, dear countrymen, wonder what this may mean."

"This will be the bit about you, mum."

"I suppose."

"And where is Launcelot? Where indeed? Where Guinevere is," said Haw-Haw. "The war forgot. Helm and mail laid aside, hanging from the bedpost."

"Elephant garlic," said Guinevere.

"What?" asked Varley.

"For the sorrel soup," Guinevere said. "The perfect thing. Why didn't I think of it before?"

"Yes, that would be nice, mum."

"Guinevere is a good woman, at heart," said the radio.

"How does he know?"

"But women are often confused," said Haw-Haw. "Also, she's getting older. Very often, when women get older, they get a little reckless."

"Not reckless enough," Guinevere said, finishing the apple.

"He's got a filthy mouth, that he does."

"But do the ratepayers want a queen who spends all her time drinking sloe gin while dallying with one of their king's chief advisers? I think not."

"What time is it?" Guinevere asked.

"Almost ten," said Varley.

"Time for the other one. See if you can get Ezra."

Varley fiddling with the radio.

"This is not my favorite among our wars," Guinevere said. "Too many competing interests. Nothing clear about it. Except that we are on God's side, of course. The thing I have always admired about Arthur is that he always manages to be on the side of the right. But Jesu, the intrigue! Once upon a time the men went out and bashed each other over the head for a day and a half, and that was it. Now we have ambassadors hithering and thithering, secret agreements with still more secret codicils, betrayals, reversals, stabs in the back—"

"Terrible it is, mum."

"One has to think about so many different sorts of people one never thought about before," Guinevere said. "Croats, for example. I never knew there was such a thing as a Croat before this war."

"Are they on our side?"

"As I understand it, they are being held in reserve for a possible uprising in the event that the Serbs fail to live up to some agreement or other."

"What's a Serb, mum?"

"I stand before you in the most perfect ignorance," said the queen. "All I know is that they share territory with the Croats. Uneasily, I gather. And then we have to worry about the Bulgarians and Rumanians and Hungarians and Albanians and God knows what all. It's enough to brast one's pate."

"Oh my," Varley said. "I forgot."

"Forgot what?"

"That man was here again today."

"What man?"

"The Pole."

"What did he want?"

"Something about the shipyards. The men in the shipyards are unhappy, he said."

"The men in the shipyards are always unhappy."

"The railwaymen too, he said. The railwaymen have done something awful."

"What?"

"He said they have welded a locomotive to the rails on the line between Ipswich and Stowmarket. So nothing can move on that line."

"That's ingenious."

"I said you were at your prayers, mum."

"And soon I shall be. You can't find Ezra?"

"There's a lot of noise, mum."

"Ezra to a T," said the queen. "Chuck it, then. I am not reckless. And thirty-six is hardly old, would you say, Varley?"

"Quite young, from where I sit."

"How old are you, Varley?"

"No one knows, mum. Close to fifty, at a guess."

"You are a handsome older woman," said the queen, "and a good friend, as well."

"Thank you, mum."

"I suppose I had better send Arthur a wire about the damn locomotive welded to the damn tracks," Guinevere said. "Did the Pole say what the railwaymen want?"

"More money, he said."

"*Quel* surprise," said the queen.

HE BOLSHEVIK anti-morale," said Ezra, "comes out of the Talmud, which is the dirtiest teaching that any race ever codified. The Talmud is the one and only begetter of the Bolshevik system."

"In a moment he'll be talking about 'kikified usurers,'" said Arthur. "One expects poets to be mad, but—"

"He reminds me," said Sir Kay, "of some old country squire, in Surrey somewhere, running on after dinner to his poor bedraggled wife."

"I suppose one could knit to this," Arthur said. "It would induce concentration."

"You would do better to inoculate your children with typhus and syphilis," said Ezra, "than to let in the Sassoons, Rothschilds, and Warburgs."

"See if you can get something else," said the king. "Or better, shut it off. I can remember when we didn't have any damned radio clattering at us day and night."

"I heard some Schoenberg, just the other day. The Suite for Piano."

"I have never understood your taste in music, dear Sir Kay. Nor the queen's. Guinevere likes music with much dolor in it. The most dolorous.

As if life didn't contain enough. I like music that is rather more affirmative, if I may put it that way."

"Queens are usually quite conservative, musically speaking," said Sir Kay. "I've known a good many, and most of them go for the old war-horses. I've never known a queen who could stand Bruckner. Play them a bit of Mahler and they fall into a pout."

"Queens get so few chances to express themselves," said Arthur. "They save them up to spend on something important."

"By the way," said Sir Kay. "There's one missing. Fiona, Queen of Gore. There was a bulletin on the teletype."

"Where is Gore?"

"Don't recall. In the north somewhere. In any case, she's been out of pocket for some weeks."

"Has she a husband? How old is she?"

"She's twenty-two. The king's quite a bit older. Named Unthank."

"She's probably out misbehaving. Try to keep it from the papers. I don't know why I should have to worry about such things when there's a war on."

"They say she's quite lovely."

"That's interesting."

"One of the most beautiful women in the realm, they say."

"That's interesting."

"Said to have a remarkable figger."

"I have put such things behind me, more or less. You know that."

"Of course, sire. Just bringing you up to date."

"Is there anything else?"

"Gawain has swapped off a damosel's head. By accident. Again."

"God in heaven," said Arthur. "Who was it?"

"A daughter of King Zog. Her name was Lynet, I believe."

"Then we'll have Albania up in arms," said Arthur. "All the hatred the Albanians have for the Italians, wasted. Gawain always gets them on the rebound, the damosels. He makes a stroke, the stroke bounces off his opponent's cuirass or whatever and detaches the head of the lady standing nearby. It's happened far too often. Doesn't make us look good in the press. Haw-Haw has been commenting on it."

"No one pays any attention to Haw-Haw."

"I quite disagree with you," said Arthur. "People hang upon his every word. They find him delicious. The entire English-speaking world believes that Launcelot is sleeping with Guinevere."

"Oh, I doubt it," said Sir Kay. "She's thirty-six. Do people still sleep with women when they're that age?"

"Each to his own taste," said the king. "I have not lain with Guinevere these dozen years. Not that I'm not fond of her, you understand. But twenty-four is my absolute upper limit. Always was and always will be."

"Quite sound," said Sir Kay. "Perhaps it's a sort of pietistic relationship, Launcelot and the queen. Perhaps they read improving works together, go to early mass together, make novenas, things of that nature."

"Guinevere has no more religion than a cat."

"There are also letters from Victor Emmanuel," said Sir Kay.

"I've read them. Most unpleasant. The Italians want Yugoslavia, Greece, Nice, and Lord knows what else."

"In the old days," said Sir Kay, "we'd have made the messenger eat the letters. Including the seals."

"I have never abused messengers," said Arthur. "I think that's rather low."

"We have a wire from the queen. Something about a locomotive welded to the tracks by the railway union."

"Yes yes yes," said Arthur. "Who is the chief of the railwaymen now? I assume they want more money."

"As do the men in the shipyards. There's a Pole who's been speaking for both groups. I forget his name."

"Give them a bit more money," said Arthur, "and raise the tax on a pint commensurately."

"No," said Sir Kay. "Increase the tax first, then

give them the rise, that's the ticket. It's less obvious."

"They think I'm made of money," said Arthur. "The supply of money is finite. They don't realize that. They think I have great strongboxes filled with money in all the cupboards and attics of all my castles."

"And so you do," said Sir Kay.

"But that's not the point," Arthur said. "That money is not *mine* in any real sense. It's the state's money, England's money. We need it to keep the country going. Who knows what may happen in this war? We may lose. We may have to ransom ourselves, or the whole bloody kingdom. It's only prudent to keep a bit laid by for contingencies. The man in the street never worries about contingencies."

"True enough."

"Besides which, Wilhelmina of the Netherlands is richer than I am, everyone knows that. Do I complain about being only the second-richest person in Europe? I do not. I accept the fact with a good grace."

"You are famously modest and prudent," said Sir Kay, "as well as a steadfast—"

"Shall we give the Italians some part of what they want? I think not. They'll only be back."

"We could bomb Milan. A preemptive strike. Make them reflect on things. Last things."

"I have never acquired a taste for bombing civilian populations," said the king. "It seems a violation of the social contract. We're supposed to do the fighting, and they're supposed to pay for it."

"Those were the days."

"Let me confess something," Arthur said. "I have always been worried about what kind of an obituary I'm going to get from *The Times*. Isn't that curious? I find it curious. How many pages? How many photographs? Of what size? Despicable, don't you think?"

"We all wonder," said Sir Kay. "We've been reading the obituaries for so long."

"If we had gone to war over Czechoslovakia," Arthur said, "we could have won then and there, I'm convinced of it. Hindsight, I suppose, but still—"

"It was the French who were frightened."

"Always correct to blame the French for things," said Arthur, "but Munich was mainly our doing. We left a great many decisions to the civil government."

"An error, in hindsight."

"The constitutional monarchy," Arthur said, "is all very well in peacetime. In peacetime one doesn't want to worry about the balance of trade and that sort of thing, one wants to go hawking. Wartime is different. Wartime needs us. Think of the siege of Andorra. We were magnificent. Launcelot inside the castle, leading the defense. He was incomparable, as always. You should have seen him on the battlements, hurling hives of bees down at the besiegers. He loves hurling hives of bees down at the besiegers. We lost, of course."

"Who bungled it?" asked Sir Kay. "Whitehall. Civilians. We're losing the war."

"We're certainly not winning it. I'm terribly tempted to have a look at Merlin's Prophecy and see how the thing turns out."

"I thought Merlin's Prophecy had been discredited."

"Of course," said Arthur. "Discredited. Thoroughly refuted. Of no scholarly interest whatsoever. Its provenance in tatters. *Which* Merlin's Prophecy are you speaking of?"

"There's more than one?"

"There's the one Geoffrey of Monmouth sent to the Bishop of Lincoln," said Arthur. "That's the famous one. Then there's the real one."

"There's a second Merlin's Prophecy?"

"There is."

"And you have it?"

"I do."

"How do you know the one you have is the real one?"

"You forget," said Arthur, "that I knew Merlin. Geoffrey of Monmouth didn't. If you are a connoisseur of vatic behavior, which I am—"

"Boo to a goose," said Sir Kay. "I'm confused."

"Further confusions await," said Arthur. "For example: If I guide myself by the Prophecy, that is to say, read the Prophecy as history even though history not yet accomplished, then the future is, for me, overdetermined, a thing I don't want. It's a matter of using it judiciously, don't you see. Using it rather than being used by it."

"Still," said Sir Kay, "if it's the actual, authentic Prophecy, it would be difficult to ignore, it seems to me."

"There's an art to it," Arthur said. "Ignoring advice, I mean. Some people never learn it."

"Can I see it?" asked Sir Kay. "The, uh, document?"

"Some people don't believe in a thing unless they've seen it with their own eyes," said Arthur. "Some people can see a thing with their own eyes and still not know what they've seen. Some people can be told something by a king and still want to see that something with their own eyes."

"Stupid of me," said Sir Kay.

"Yes," said Arthur.

AUNCELOT locked in combat with the Black Knight.

The Black Knight's armor is black plate chased with silver. Launcelot deals him a mighty buffet upon the shoulder.

"Sir, do you yield?"

"Heaven forfend," said the Black Knight.

"Would you care to rest, just for a moment?"

"You are an ever-courteous knight," said the Black Knight, "and yes, I could do with a moment's surcease."

The two sitting together, their helms removed, sharing a bit of Brie-with-pepper on pebble bread.

"The way I see it," said the Black Knight, "the basic problem is Russia."

"That's what they say," said Launcelot. "I wonder."

"My feeling is that Germany intends to launch a Russian campaign."

"When?"

"They're amassing battles on the frontier, so I'm told."

"Is your information reliable?"

"As reliable as anything you get at my level,"

said the Black Knight. "Somewhat better than what the newspapers have, somewhat worse than is available in the ministries. They tell us ordinary knights as little as possible. You, on the other hand, have access to the king."

"Formerly," said Launcelot. "Not now. Arthur loves me still, I think, but God wot I have not seen him these many months. It's the Guinevere thing."

"I've heard about it," the Black Knight said. "It's broadcast everywhere. It's almost more important than the war itself, in terms of public interest."

"Once upon a time," said Launcelot, "one could have a love affair in decent quietude. Adultery used to be a private matter, just the principals worrying about it. Now one can't pop open a French letter without being plastered all over the hoardings."

"I knew a girl once in Greece," said the Black Knight. "I was sick unto the depths of my soul."

"I've never been to Greece. An island, isn't it?"

"Many islands. Sweet Jesu, but she put me out of countenance. Wouldn't have me because I was black."

"You *are* black," said Launcelot. "Black, but comely."

"Where I come from," said the Black Knight, "everyone is black. As far as the eye can see. White people are regarded as freaks of nature. The sight of

a white person causes cows to birth poisonous shrubs."

"What country is that?"

"Dahomey."

"Don't know it. How's the food?"

"Not too bad. My mother used to make a cassava pie I still dream about."

"In this country, gossip seems the principal export sometimes. One must guard one's reputation with an iron hand."

"I've always wondered," said the Black Knight, "what sort of play the press will give the story when I depart."

"I took the precaution, some time ago," said Launcelot, "of sitting down with the chap who does *The Times* obituaries. Chap named Hackett, not at all a bad fellow."

"That was enterprising."

" 'Hackett,' I said to him, 'if a thing is worth doing, it's worth doing well.' He seemed to agree with me. Nervous little man, jumpy, one might say —I could not make out what was making him dither so. Finally he asked if I would mind removing my mace from the table. We were in a pub, the Lamb and Flag, and I had placed my mace on the table. I had just come in from the field, and the mace was, truth to tell, a bit bloody. 'Well, I'll put it somewhere,' I said to him. 'Please,' he said. I looked around for a peg to hang it on, but the place was pegless. So I put it in the men's room, stood it in a corner there. My second-best mace. I said to myself, 'I'll wager a horse that some rascal steals the bloody thing,' no pun intended.

"So Hackett had calmed down a bit, he was well into his second gin, I might add, and I explained the position. It was not, I said, that I took a specially exalted view of my life; it was a life like many another, with its good times and bad times and periods of inanition. *But*, I said to him, and here there was a slight contretemps, for I found that I had been pounding the table for emphasis and that I had a rather large dagger in my hand, I don't know why, habit I suppose, and that I had hacked through the table. So I pulled over another table, dislodging a pair of louts who had been drinking there, and wiped Hackett off—he had got a lapful of gin—and ordered us another round, and tried to remember the point I had been making. Hackett asked if I minded if he telephoned his wife. I said yes, I did."

"You were firm with him."

"Yes, I was. I told him that although my life had been in many ways a life like many another, in other ways it had been quite *unlike* many another, because of the peculiar circumstances of my birth, class, and history. I then explained chivalry to him, more or less, the short form of course, gave him some notion of my early days, filled him in on the sociology of my father's kingdom and of the several realms I have inhabited since I left it, outlined the art of war (very sketchily indeed, for I did not wish to give him more than he could handle), and listed for him my chief exploits since the age of seven. He was taking notes quite feverishly, damned fine notes —I had him read them back to me every quarter hour or so, in the interest of accuracy."

"Quite proper."

"I think so. About Guinevere (or any other lady) I told him nothing, for that sort of thing, in my view, has no place in a proper memorial. I told him that I was aware that photographs accompanying *obits*, as he called them, in his paper were run either one-, two-, or three-column and said I would prefer the three-column, and furnished him with a very good one lately taken by an excellent practitioner at Joyous Gard. Hackett was most grateful to have it and for all the time I had given him, and departed with many expressions of admiration and respect."

"Jolly good."

"In sum," Launcelot said, "the press is not difficult to manage if one exhibits a certain intellectual rigor. My mace was in fact stolen on this occasion."

"The devil you say."

"Sir Knight," said Launcelot, "I wouldn't mind having you in our camp."

"I'm rather a free lance," said the Black Knight, "by temperament. But you are such a valiant and worshipful knight and well-met fellow that I wouldn't mind at all enlisting under your banner."

"Well," said Launcelot, "I think you are a rare fellow, valiant, comely, and well-spoken, and I would be enormously pleased to list you on our rolls."

"I think the thing is done," said the Black Knight, and they rose to their feet and clasped each other in their arms, and tears brast out of their eyen, and they fell to the ground in a swoon.

LYONESSE sleeping under a tree, one knee raised.

The lieutenant unbuttoning her shirt.

Lyonesse shifts position. Hand on her head.

The lieutenant unbuckling her belt.

"I've won cups for this," Lyonesse said. "Silver cups."

"Cups?"

"Prizes," said Lyonesse. "Are you sure you're up to it?"

The lieutenant sitting with his back against a tree. "You are a something," he said.

"I like a bit more wooing," Lyonesse said. "Although you are a fine-looking fellow, I'll give you that."

"Stuff it."

"You can have my stripes."

"Good Lord," he said, "I don't want your silly stripes. And I know one shouldn't, strictly speaking, make passes at the NCOs. But I didn't expect you."

"You're a baby," said Lyonesse. "I've got more time in the mess queue than you've got in the army."

"Very possibly true," said Edward. "And I can't read a map, and battalion wouldn't have given me a platoon if they'd had anybody else at all. Still, you're stuck with me, for a bit."

"It's a very large war," said Lyonesse, "something for everybody."

"I had understood," Edward said, "that there were to be no women in combat units."

"I fell through the cracks," said Lyonesse. "There are others in other units. No one's complained up to now."

"You're carried on the rolls as a medic."

"I am a medic. Among other things."

"How do you like to be wooed, as you put it?"

Edward handing her a white clover blossom.

"No no no," she said, "too tentative, a bit more dash. Have you no champagne?"

"No champagne."

"Butter, then. If you truly want the troops to love you, you'll sally forth and bag some butter. Quite a dry potato I had for lunch."

"I don't want them to love me. If they merely suspend judgement for a few weeks, I'll be more than satisfied. I can give you some cognac."

He fished in his rucksack.

"Never thought I'd spend my time bucking up a sprog lieutenant," Lyonesse said.

"What sergeants are for, I thought."

"Perhaps I shouldn't ask, but what did you do before? Before OTC?"

"You won't laugh."

"I won't laugh."

"I was a plasterer."

"What's that?"

"Chap that slaps plaster on a wall and then smooths it out with a trowel."

"Must take a great deal of skill."

"A degree of skill."

"You're very well-spoken, for a laboring man."

"Thank you. I had a bit of schooling here and there, thank God. But nothing that made me employable."

"Do plasterers do well in the world?"

"One of the better-paid trades. Got paid then a bit more than I get paid now."

"I see no reason lieutenants should live in luxury. There are so many of them."

"Right."

"Probably fifty thousand or sixty thousand just in our own forces."

"Taking into account all branches."

"Mostly new-minted. From among the educable."

"I consider myself educable."

"Yes, you seem educable. Up to a point. And then there are the things you already know."

"Plastering, for example."

"I was thinking more of your drinking habits. The cognac."

"Otard XO. Not too bad."

"Is there more?"

"More might be found."

"Would you be encouraged by a kiss?"

"Encouraged to do what?"

"Find more cognac."

"I think I would, rather."

Back into the rucksack.

"I am tired of this war," said Edward. "Also I don't understand it. It seems most un-Christian."

"They're Christians too," said Lyonesse. "Catholics and Protestants, much like us."

"Why are we fighting them?"

"They're mad. We're sane."

"How do we know?"

"That we're sane?"

"Yes."

"Am I sane?"

"To all appearances."

"And you, do you consider yourself sane?"

"I do."

"Well, there you have it."

"But don't they also consider themselves sane?"

"I think they know. Deep down. That they're not sane."

"How must that make them feel?"

"Terrible, I should think. They must fight ever more fiercely, in order to deny what they know to be true. That they are not sane."

"That's very shrewd," Edward said. "I shouldn't wonder if you were right."

"Yes," said Lyonesse, taking off her shirt. "Lie with me."

"With all my heart."

25

UINEVERE said: "I've had quite enough of this. I've sat here embroidering pillowcases quite long enough. It's May, and I will go a-Maying, war or no war."

"But this is the seat of government," said Mordred. "If you leave, constitutionally there'll be no one in charge."

"There's Parliament. There's the prime minister."

"Yes, but they're not symbols. You're a symbol. Symbolically, we need a royal here."

"Then you do it," said Guinevere. "You're royal enough for the purpose. Not quite top drawer, of course, but Arthur's son, nevertheless."

"As the queen wishes."

"Do you think thirty-six is old?"

"Not *so* old," said Mordred. "Rather old. Old for what purpose?"

"Never mind," said the queen. "I'll need a few knights to ride along with me. Half a dozen will be ample. Varley will come, as usual, and we'll need servants. I'll take the good cook and leave you the second best. You don't care, do you?"

"No matter."

"Arthur does love his venison pie, and nobody does venison pie like Charles. Assuming I run into Arthur. Launcelot likes venison pie as well. I suppose we'd better take a gamekeeper or two, to harvest the venison."

"Perhaps a small orchestra?"

"Mordred, you needn't be sour. I am quite aware that this is wartime. I have at least fought at the side of my husband."

"The queen's courage is not in question."

"But yours is, and that's what you're so sour about. Get out in the field with the troops. Take a buffet or two. You're unscarred, that's what makes you suspect. A slashed cheek or a broken pate would go a long way toward making you—"

"One of the boys?"

"Well, yes," said Guinevere.

"The thrust above the breast you received at Poitiers has gone to your head, madam."

"A lucky wound," Guinevere agreed. "Quite minor. Still, I bled. It shows good will, if you take my meaning."

"It's theatre," said Mordred. "These great hulking heroes—Arthur, Launcelot, Gawain, Gareth—come back to the castle all bloodied up, and people throw their hats in the air."

"Yes," said Guinevere, "they win much worship. Not quite theatre. Real pain. People respect that."

"I am delighted to be lectured on the manly virtues by my father's wife," said Mordred. "Perhaps the queen is as eloquent on the womanly. May we expect a little ballade on honesty, a little scherzo on fidelity?"

"You *are* a bastard," said Guinevere. "If I had anyone else to leave the kingdom in care of, I would pick him. Now give me the pleasure of your speedy departure, sir. I'll have the documents drawn and sent to you."

"Madam," said Mordred, and withdrew.

"Well," said Guinevere, "what do you think of that?"

Launcelot stepping from behind the arras.

"I think he is a cankered man," he said. "Are you not taking a great risk in giving over to him the privy seal and suchlike?"

"He'll enjoy the feeling for a bit," said the queen. "I don't think he'll do anything terrible immediately."

"Ill will," Launcelot went on, "is usually, in my experience, the result of some action by another. In Mordred's case, it sort of sprays out in all directions. It may be that he realizes that Arthur does not love him. Although Arthur always tries to be as evenhanded as possible, in dealing with his children."

Launcelot removing Guinevere's blouse.

"A kiss," he said. "I've been so long away. How nicely you've healed."

"Not much of a something," said the queen, sitting on his lap. "And Arthur got the fellow with as neat a backhand as I've seen in my whole three and thirty years."

"Six and thirty, isn't it?"

"You have a good memory, God wot. Don't you ever forget things?"

"I forget as much as I can," said Launcelot.

"Me?"

"You are the great curse and the great joy of my life," said Launcelot.

"Which is paramount?"

"In that I wish to be justified in God's sight," said Launcelot, "a curse. In that I wished to find and have found my soul's twin, a joy."

"Arthur's quite . . . disturbed, you know."

"I know nothing of the sort. He's worried about the war, of course, as who is not? But beyond that, beyond the natural gray pallor of worry, sometimes tinged with red, that sits upon his brow, red when anger intrudes, gray most of the time, but when the weather, say, is unfavorable to our designs in this part of the world or that part of the world, as laid out upon the giant wall map that dominates his headquarters, then red—"

"I am merely his wife," said Guinevere, "merely the queen who knows him best in the whole world."

"Granted."

"Even at great distances I notice things."

"What things?"

"When he chants—"

"What sort of *chant*? I've never heard him *chant*."

29

"You've never slept with him."

"I certainly have not."

"Well, he chants in his sleep. Some people clatter in their sleep, through the nose. Arthur chants in his sleep. Ancient chants."

"So?"

"Even at great distances, I hear him chanting. In the middle of the night."

"That's passing strange. If I may say so."

"Indeed. Well, the matter of the chant has changed. Now he asks for strength. Always before he's *had* strength, don't you see. That's the difference."

"I don't like it."

"No more do I."

NOBLE lady bathing alone in a forest pool!"

"She has shed her garments, every garment!"

"She is of surpassing beauty! Skin of the purest alabaster!"

"Too much blue in it to be alabaster! Alabaster ranges from yellowish-pinkish to pinkish-grayish!"

"This is a kind of Delft! Traces of blue in the white!"

"Skin most royal-looking! Surely that is the queen, Guinevere, bathing there!"

"Were it Guinevere, there'd be ladies of the court dawdling about!"

"What place is this?"

"I know not, but it is hard by the poor hut where Nacien the hermit gathers worts!"

"Perhaps the ladies of the court are sampling the beer Nacien brews from his worts!"

"Look you how the sunlight, pouring through the leaves of the trees, dapples the beauteous stomach with irregular shapes as if leaves had been painted there by some great leaf-painter like Bouguereau or de Heem!"

"De Heem?"

"And look you how her long white legs sparkle

in the light as she abrades them with switches so that the blue will more pronounce itself against the white!"

"With a willing heart, had I not already defouled my soul in deadly sin by this same act of looking!"

"God wot it feels like sin!"

"And surely mortal, naked majesty being a thing most rare and terrible!"

"Now she stands upon a rock, the better to let the sun disport upon her shoulders, breasts, and buttocks! How young she looks! How supple! How lusty! She could be thirty!"

"I think nine and twenty!"

"No, eight and twenty!"

"Here are her handmaidens, bearing robes of a hundred colors!"

"They braid the golden hair and set great jeweled combs therein!"

"They girdle the divine form in poppy-red and puce, apricot and ocher, heliotrope and mauve!"

"A shawmist and a hurdy-gurdier appear and ply their instruments most sweetly in the forest air!"

"Music carpets the forest floor with little sheaves of dead or dying notes!"

"Sweet Jesu, what a day!"

AUNCELOT and the Black Knight, Roger de Ibadan, trotting through Pembroke Forest.

"I wasn't aware that there *were* any knights in Africa," said Launcelot. "Of course I've never been there."

"We are few," said Sir Roger. "It's a matter of military technology, really. The region has a long tradition of metalworking. Our sculptors are especially fine. If you visit the British Museum, you'll find quite a wonderful collection of Benin figures, as they're called, mostly done by the lost-wax process but also a good many in hammered iron."

"Went to a museum once, in Paris," Launcelot said. "Lots of pictures and statues and that sort of thing."

"The Louvre, doubtless."

"God wot I was plumb wore out. Never did get to the end of it."

"The Benin kings encouraged metalworking in all its forms," said Sir Roger. "When you get metalworkers of high competence, it's just a step to the manufacture of armor. When you get armor, you get knights. It's like the stirrup. Certain kinds of mounted combat would be impossible without the stirrup. Unites the strength of the man with the strength of the horse."

"Never thought about it," said Launcelot. "I thought saddles had always had stirrups."

"First appeared in North Korea in the fifth century," said Sir Roger. "Books have been written about the influence of the stirrup on warfare. Not that I've ever read one. The thing about books is, there are quite a number you don't have to read."

"Never been much of a one for books," said Launcelot.

"I've read a great many," said Sir Roger. "When you're black, everyone tends to assume you're stupid. So I take care not to be stupid. Read a good one just the other day, *The Anatomy of Melancholy,* by Burton. A jewel of a book."

"Don't know it."

" 'Diogenes struck the father when the son swore,' " Sir Roger quoted. "Now that's wisdom."

"My father never struck me," said Launcelot. "On the other hand, he never spoke to me, either."

"Your father was King Ban of Benwick."

"How did you know that?"

"The whole world knows," said Sir Roger. "I ask you to consider the implications of the name 'Ban.' "

"I have," said Launcelot. "The name was on the mark. He was a good man and a good king, but proscriptive in the extreme. He liked to forbid things. This was forbidden, that was forbidden, the other was forbidden. Wake up in the morning and you'd find that three new things had been forbidden. Not the jolliest place in the world, Benwick."

"Something we have in common," said Sir Roger. "*My* father was a judge. Wrote many opinions, many many opinions—a most opinionated fellow. Sometimes wrote opinions in cases where he wasn't asked for one. Still, it kept him busy and contented."

"What's that up there?" asked Launcelot, pointing.

"Appears to be a man," said Sir Roger. "Clothed in rags and tatters and leaning upon a staff."

"A poacher, I'll wager."

Launcelot spurring his horse forward.

"You, sirrah," he said to the man. "What might your business be in the king's forest? And are those the king's rabbits I spy slung round your neck?"

"Formerly God's rabbits," said the man calmly. "Soon to be my dinner."

"Know you not," said Launcelot, "that taking rabbits in the king's forest will earn you forty strokes per rabbit?"

"I am a man of God," said the stranger, "and thus care nothing for earthly prohibitions."

"What is your name, insolent fellow?"

"I am Walter the Penniless," said the man, "and I preach the great crusade."

"What crusade is that?"

"A new crusade," said Walter, "against the enemies of Our Lord right here in Europe."

"A crusade in Europe," said Launcelot. "I take it by 'enemies' you intend the Teutons and so forth."

"Maybe I do and maybe I don't," said Walter the Penniless. "Sit with me awhile and I will tell you my ideas."

Launcelot making a fire from twigs and branches. Sir Roger skinning the rabbits.

"The way I see it," said Walter the Penniless, "the old order is dead. Finished. We don't want the extraordinary, as represented by you gentlemen and your famous king, any longer. It is a time for the unexceptional, the untalented, the ordinary, the downright maladroit. Quite a large constituency. All genuine certified human beings, with hearts and souls and all the rest of it. You fellows, worshipful as you may be, are anachronisms. You know what happened when the Polish cavalry attacked the German tanks. Why, the horsemen were smashed to flitters! A tank is nothing else but an expression of the will of the hundred workers who put it together. And they shall prevail!"

"Good rabbit," said Sir Roger, chewing.

"Could do with a bit of dill," said Launcelot.

"Have you ever had roebuck?"

"Can't say that I have."

"Roast of roebuck with canna berries," said Sir Roger. "Now there's a dish."

"I suppose you dash weird and strange African spices all over it."

"We have a few little tricks," said Roger. "There's a thing called mui-mui, which is ground-up mui root mixed with chopped tree frog, that's pretty potent—"

"We have plans for you, the warrior class," said Walter the Penniless. "Your functions, in the future, will be chiefly ornamental. Ushers, traffic wardens, overseers of car parks, doormen, elevator operators, that sort of thing. Little niches where you can do no harm. Not the life you've led heretofore but not, on the whole, a bad life."

"This fellow seems a bit Red to me," said Sir Roger.

"I've never met one," said Launcelot. "A Red."

"Africa has a fair number of Reds, and they sound very much like this fellow."

"I do know," said Launcelot, "that I'm damned tired of hearing about the Polish cavalry."

"I get a sense that we're wasting our time," said Sir Roger. "That we should be out slaying dragons or something."

"You don't bump into them all that often," Launcelot said. "Very few people in this world have actually slain a dragon. You will find a dozen vaunters in any great hall who claim to have done so, and the minstrels sing of many such triumphs, but what has actually been slain, in almost every case, is a lizard."

"Lizard?"

"Typically the Eyed or Jewelled Lizard, found in Spain, Italy, the south of France, and our own country, and which may attain a length of two feet. A largish lizard, but not a dragon."

"I see."

"One understands that a man does not wish to come home to his castle of an evening and say to his lady, 'God wot I had the fight of me life today —no sooner had I fewtered my spear than the monster was upon me,' and have the lady say, 'But, good Sir Giles' or 'But, good Sir Hebes,' and then have the awful question come, 'What manner of monster was it?' and be forced to reply, 'Lizard.' "

"Quite."

"True dragons are Danish and speak Danish, a tongue the Danes themselves describe as less a language than a throat disease. To attract a dragon, one chains a naked maiden to a rock. The maiden must be chained to the rock in such a way that every part of her is visible to the dragon. Many famous paintings demonstrate the technique; Ingres's *Angelica Saved by Ruggiero* is an example. After the dragon has inspected your maiden to its heart's content, you issue one of the conventional formal challenges, in Danish—*Jeg udfordre dig til ridderlig camp*' is the way one usually puts it—and then the fight begins."

"Extraordinary."

"If a mixture of flame and Danish comes from

the creature and your armor is singed black, you know that you have not been fighting a lizard."

"Amazing."

"I have slain upwards of thirty authentic dragons, but I told *The Times* fellow not to put that in the paper."

"Furthermore," said Walter the Penniless, "have you noticed what the king's been up to lately? Been acting a little strange, Arthur, hasn't he? Have you chaps been paying attention? Or is he just too noble and grand to answer for his actions like other kings?"

"Shall we brast his pate or give him a few pennies?" asked Sir Roger.

"The latter, I think. Deprive him of his rationale. I've got two pounds six."

"I've got three pounds."

The knights showering money on Walter the Penniless.

UINEVERE at a canter, Maying in woods and meadows, all clad in green, bedashed with herbs, mosses, and flowers, in great joy and delights.

The Brown Knight appears.

"Stand," the Brown Knight said.

Two of Guinevere's party, Sir Dodinas le Savage and Sir Ironside of the Red Lands, charging the Brown Knight. The Brown Knight's sword flashing.

"Ah, they are smitten to the earth with grimly wounds," said Guinevere. "Who is this miscreant knight?"

Sir Griflet le Fise de Dieu and Sir Galleron of Galway engaging the Brown Knight, who puts sore hurt upon them.

"My knights are being bashed to flitters," Guinevere said. "Where is Launcelot when I need him? Off somewhere pursuing additional worship. He already has more worship than any knight in the known world, and still he roams, seeking further opportunities to add to his worship. If I didn't know him so well, I'd think him unsure of himself. On the other hand, one relishes the opportunity to do what one does well, such as inflicting mortal hurt upon the enemy. Still—"

A great cry arising. A new knight hurtling upon the field, clad all in plain gray armor.

The Brown Knight recoiling.

"You, sir," he said, "are you who I think you are?"

The new knight said nothing.

"Loose your helm, sir, so that I can see your face. For if you are Launcelot du Lac, then I will surrender and place myself under your protection. But if you are just an ordinary knight, then I will brast your pate."

"You first," said the newcome knight. "Remove your helm, so that I can see who it is that makes free with the queen's escort, that bore you no ill and had nothing more in mind than freshful Maying on this May day."

The Brown Knight removing his helm. The new knight spurring his horse forward and giving the other many great strokes upon the visage with the flat of his sword.

"Can't be Launcelot," the queen said, "for this is tricherie, and Launcelot does not countenance tricherie in any form. Still, I am glad that this new knight has whacked that fellow to the ground, where he now writhes in hurt."

"Launcelot would never pull a filthy trick like that," said Sir Bedevere, at the queen's elbow. "Even on a knight so brazen as to wear brown armor with a black horse. Still, I am glad the fellow's down, because he fought as one enchafed by a fiend."

"Quite so," said the queen. "But the one in gray has trotted off, and what in the world shall we do with this one?"

"I see two possibilities," said Sir Bedevere. "We can kill him, or we can persuade him into your service."

"Fetch him, then," said Guinevere, "and we'll see which he prefers."

The Brown Knight brought, his visage in flitters.

"Sir Knight," said the queen, "why have you rashed my people so? That were only Maying in a pleasant fashion, seeking the freshness of the season, and that you put great rasure upon, and broached their flesh with divers thrusts, and so on and so on? That had not that new champion, he of the rather plain armor, entered upon the scene, my very self had been at forfeit?"

"Madam," said the Brown Knight, "I knew not that it was the queen's party I addressed, but thought it, rather, a party of the enemy that had got behind our lines and disguised itself as good English knights and true, for the bafflement of simple folk, because I did not figger that anybody would be out Maying in wartime, without a care in the world, when the whole world is embroiled in a most monstrous struggle, whose outcome will determine, for good or ill—"

43

"Enchafed by a fiend," said Sir Bedevere, "in the rhetorical dimension also."

"Are you suggesting I'm frivolous, Sir Knight?" said Guinevere. "I take it ill indeed if that be the burthen of your speech, for look you, just because a person goes Maying in Maytime, because of a restlessness in the blood entirely appropriate, in my view, to the season, that does not mean—"

"It's catching," said Bedevere. "You're as bad as he is."

The Brown Knight kneeling.

"Tell me the name of the knight who bested me," he said. "Because although he bested me by gullery and fiddle, in the main, still the buffets he dealt me bespoke a strong arm, the like of which I have not met with in my six and twenty years."

"We know not," said Guinevere. "Tell me, Brown Knight, where do you hail from?"

"Scotland," said the knight. "We like brown in Scotland, it is the color of our whiskey and the color of our cloth and the color of our heaths when the sun has done with them. And although I am aware that knights of good pedigree should not wear brown armor with a black horse, I do as I please, mostly. Brown is also the most sexual of colors, as many learned works have established, this being so, in my opinion, because of its relation, in terms of the color wheel, to lort—I use the Danish term so as not to offend the queen's . . ."

Guinevere in conversation with the Brown Knight.

"The bombing has been most terrible," he said. "I have lately come from London, where there are fires everywhere. They're sending over five and six hundred planes at a crack. The people are taking it very well, considering everything."

"But aren't we also bombing them?" asked Guinevere.

"Yes," said the Brown Knight. "We've been using Wellingtons, Hampdens, and Halifaxes against their cities. Losses are high, though. Running about six or seven percent per raid. That's very close to unacceptable."

"What *is* unacceptable?"

"One never says what unacceptable *is*," said the Brown Knight. "It varies, you see, according to the situation. The situation might require your one day declaring that what is acceptable is greater, you see, than what had previously been unacceptable. A trap you don't wish to fall into. That's why we use the formula 'very close to unacceptable.' "

"A ghastly way to fight a war," said Guinevere. "I much prefer the old ways."

"I don't disagree," said the Brown Knight. "War should be left to the warriors, that is to say, us."

"The reason it's not," Guinevere said, "is that you knights are forever mucking about in the woods banging each other to pieces. You have no sense of the long-range plan, no strategic sense."

"It's our tradition," said the Brown Knight. "It's how we accumulate worship."

"Well and good," said Guinevere, "and I admit I like to see a well-placed buffet on the helm or thrust to the groin as much as any man. But these days that sort of behavior doesn't, as they say, cut the mustard. What is one knight on horseback, however accomplished, to six hundred aircraft engaged in precision bombing? Not much."

"They are anything but precise," said the Brown Knight. "They do a lot of damage, yes, but *precise* they're not. They smash the teapot and miss the petrol dump."

"Is that true?"

"Too true. I was a pilot once. I gave it up because while individual air combat has some of the attributes of knightly encounter, it's just not the same. The machine gun is not a comely weapon."

Guinevere in bed with the Brown Knight.

"Wonderful," said the queen, "quite the best I've ever had."

"We Scots know a thing or two," said Sir Robert. "By the Clyde, Forth, Dee, Tay, and Tweed, our principal rivers—I swear by our principal rivers because I do not believe in God—by the Clyde,

Forth, Dee, Tay, and Tweed, I declare that you are the best bounce I ever had in all my days."

"Charming of you," said Guinevere. "The pursuit of the orgasm is in itself, I feel, something that should be left to the lower orders, which are scanty of pleasure other than booze. But, when coupled, no pun intended, with the very highest level of spiritual affinity, as in the present case—"

"You are my kind of queen," the Brown Knight said, "even though you are thirty-six."

"Have you ever slept with a queen before?"

"I have," said the Brown Knight. "Three, in fact. I'm not boasting, I hope. You ask me, and I reply in honest, manly fashion. They were not, perhaps, queens of large domains, but queens nevertheless. You are the best."

"I have always been the best," said Guinevere, "my whole life long."

AN THAT be Mordred, dancing there, alone in the moonlight?"

"None other!"

"What's he dancing about?"

"The spectacle is so singular, so unprecedented, that we will have to read the dance!"

"He bows to the left, he bows to the right, then he bows to the front!"

"As if accepting applause!"

"Now he raises his right knee, slowly, slowly, his linked hands under the knee, and abruptly kisses it!"

"Self-love! Disgusting in the extreme!"

"He is making pushing-away motions with his two hands and kicking ones with his left foot!"

"By this he shows an alienage from the general run of folk that walk the earth!"

"He leaps, runs, leaps and runs and leaps!"

"He is vaunting himself the more!"

"Now he hops up and down on the stage, or what would be the stage an' it were a stage, with his right leg extended and his hands forming a hoop or circlet above his head!"

" 'Tis a crown he's miming!"

"Fie, fie! The rankest treason is being danced here!"

"Now he is making counting motions, placing the forefinger of his right hand on the thumb, forefinger, second finger, third finger, and little finger of his left!"

"That's England's wealth he's counting!"

"Now he mimes climbing a ladder, higher and higher and higher—"

"The very world to surmount!"

"What could have produced a mind so bent and cankered?"

"His eyes are like the heads of lisping snakes!"

"Sometimes they spit, the eyes, and sometimes they drip a kind of hairy substance—"

"Heaven forfend I should say anything that might be considered an extenuation of Mordred's conduct, but—"

"But what?"

"Arthur did attempt to kill him when he was terribly young!"

"Because Merlin had prophesied that Arthur would be destroyed by one born on May-day!"

"Arthur had all the children born on May-day, begotten of lords and born of ladies, set aboard a ship!"

"The ship sailed to the accompaniment of affirmative music!"

"Arthur does love music, every kind!"

"The ship was all to-riven on the rocks! Intentionally!"

"That borders on the perfidious!"

"But Mordred was cast up and saved!"

"And lived to become the loathsome devil that he is!"

"To think that such a man now sits in the seat of power!"

"A black day for Britain!"

"And blacker yet to come!"

LAUNCELOT whanging away at the helm of the Yellow Knight. Sharp buffets exchanged on both sides. Advantage now to this one, now to that one.

A small girl clad in green appears on the field.

"Please, sirs," she said.

Launcelot signaled the Yellow Knight to stand back. "What is it?" he said to the girl.

"Please, sir, will you buy some Girl Guide cookies? Five shillings the box."

"Four," said Launcelot, reaching for his purse.

"Four boxes?"

"Four shillings," said Launcelot. "Two boxes. One for my friend here."

"Sir, they're Girl Guide cookies. The price is fixed. We aren't allowed to change it."

"You'll lose the sale, then," said Launcelot. "I've never had a box of Girl Guide cookies that was worth more than two shillings. Four is generous."

"Oh, come now," said the Yellow Knight, Sir Colgrevaunce of Gore. "Give the girl her ten shillings, for heaven's sake."

"Four shillings a box and not a farthing more," said Launcelot, leveling his sword at Sir Colgrevaunce.

"Mercy Jesu, you're as jumpy as a bag of fleas."

"Jumpy as a bag of fleas," said Launcelot. "That's quite colorful. Something they say in Gore?"

"Coined by Pope at the height of his powers. Now I am going to give this young lady ten shillings, and you are going to have a cookie, and then we'll get back to the crashing and banging."

"Thank you, good Sir Knight," said the little girl. "Could I interest you in a pot of Girl Guide marmalade? The Persian lime's quite fine."

"Enough," said Launcelot. "You have plundered two of the greatest softheads in the realm— be content."

The girl scampered off. Sir Colgrevaunce opened the cookies.

"Tell me," said Launcelot, eating his cookie, "how go things in Gore? Is the queen still missing?"

"Aye, and the king half mad with rage," said Sir Colgrevaunce.

"Her departure was French leave?"

"Very much so. King Unthank was sleeping with one of her ladies-in-waiting. In point of fact, *all* of her ladies-in-waiting."

"How many were there?"

"A round dozen. The queen finally twigged to the situation and took herself off."

"Then he has no one to blame but himself."

"Kings are not good at blaming themselves for things, you know that."

"Arthur is," said Launcelot. "Everything awry in the world he charges to his own account."

"Arthur is a saint. Unthank is far from that."

"Unfortunate," said Launcelot. "What's the queen's name?"

"Fiona Lyonesse de Gales."

"Is she the one whose father was murdered by a giant?"

"No no, you're thinking of Fiona of the Wet Lands."

"The giant's name was Morgor. I believe I dealt with him. Had an extra eye in his left elbow. Damnedest thing I ever saw—messed up my foot-work."

"You have a reputation for taking off the left arm of your opponents. Why?"

"Leaves them the right. Usually the person's best arm. It is ever better, in my view, to leave an opponent with some shreds of his dignity and a margin of employability than to insist on every last cubic centimeter of blood."

"That's quite thoughtful."

"You fight well, Sir Knight. How goes the war, in your view?"

"Poorly," said the Yellow Knight. "I hear terrible things on every side. What do you know about Mordred?"

"A son of Arthur, more or less. He's distinguished himself thus far chiefly by his skill in speculation, currency manipulation. He dresses all in black. He's accompanied everywhere by a pair of brachets named Gad and Gisarme. He performs upon the cembalo and has written a number of compositions for it, said by the knowledgeable to be quite poor. At twelve he attempted to poison me by adding hyoscine to the beer I was drinking. The dose was miscalculated and the affair treated as a childish prank."

"You're not overfond of him."

"No."

"And this fellow Churchill seems less than competent."

"Not done very well by us thus far, that's a certainty."

"Do you think he's in the pay of the enemy? Haw-Haw suggested that just the other day."

"I never listen to the bugger. More tea?"

"Had enough, thank you."

"What's this?" said Launcelot. He unrolled a slip of paper from his box of Girl Guide cookies.

Sir Colgrevaunce peering over his shoulder.

"Appears to be a mathematical formula of some sort."

"So it does," said Launcelot, and stuck the paper in his helm. "Well, let's have at it."

They resumed the crashing and banging.

RTHUR, Sir Kay, Sir Helin le Blank, and Sir Lamorak de Gales inspecting the locomotive welded to the track.

"How does one unweld a weld?" Arthur asked. "Chip at it with a crowbar?"

"We could have them take up the track," said Sir Lamorak, "fore and aft of the engine. Then that section could be slid to one side and new rails laid. But you'd have to have a mighty powerful something to move it with."

"They could lay track perpendicular to the existing track and bring in another engine on that track," said Sir Kay, "but it would take donkey's years."

"If Merlin were still in business he could magick it away," said the king. " 'Avaunt!' he'd say, and the thing would be done. I'm afraid I never adequately appreciated Merlin." He paused. "Big bastard, isn't it."

Further inspection of the quite large locomotive.

"I say we blast," said Sir Helin. "I have with me sufficient gelignite to place said engine in nice proximity to the Isle of Wight, if you wish."

"We have upwards of sixty thousand subjects on the Isle of Wight," said Sir Kay. "Most of 'em loyal, I should say. Loyal and God-fearing. To

dump a locomotive on them in the middle of the night would be most unfortunate. Not that I doubt your skill."

"I blew nineteen bridges in France," said Sir Helin. "A neat job on each and every one; you may check my fitness reports."

"We could have the sappers tunnel beneath it," said Sir Lamorak, "and when the hole is big enough, cut the rails and the engine would fall into the pit. Then we fill in around it and lay new track. What think you?"

"If we could *melt it* somehow," replied Sir Kay. "Build a sort of furnace sort of thing around it—"

"Jack it up," said Arthur. "Remove the wheels and attached track. Replace wheels. Replace track. Lower engine, and there you have it."

"What a good idea," said Sir Lamorak. "Why didn't I think of that?"

"A splendid idea," said Sir Helin. "Clean, orderly, logical, logical-surgical, surgical-executive. . ."

"A perfect solution," Sir Kay said. "One understands, at moments like this, why you are king, sire. Your idea is fifty times better than any of our ideas."

"I wish to endorse those sentiments," said Sir Lamorak, kneeling, "with my whole heart and soul."

"*Moi aussi,*" said Sir Helin. "A true miracle of the intellect, performed before our very eyes."

"You chaps are fussing too much," said Arthur. "It's nothing more than simple everyday brilliance. Call the railway mob, and let's get on with it."

Arthur seated on an oil drum, dictating.

"As beyond my powers in the present instance."

Sir Kay looked up from his steno pad. "*Is it* beyond your powers?"

"I think so," said Arthur. "What this war has done is persuade me just how much of existence is beyond my powers. Not a pleasant experience. Did you hear Ezra this morning?"

"Missed him. Was he good?"

"First-rate. Said that Roosevelt is an imbecile and gets all his ideas from Felix Frankfurter. Called him Franklin D. Frankfurter Jewsfeld."

"Haw-Haw?"

"Haw-Haw was on about the queen again."

"Specifically?"

"I shan't repeat it. It involved the Scottish chap. Or the alleged Scottish chap."

"Um."

"I wonder if he exists. The Scottish chap."

"Um."

"In the old days I'd have had her burnt. Just on the whisper."

"And Launcelot would have come crashing in out of the blue and rescued her. Slaying half a dozen good knights in the process."

"Yes. One could always count on Launcelot. That's why I felt so free to order up the stake. Launcelot never failed me. And look at this." He handed Sir Kay a paper.

"What is it?"

"Jury duty," said Arthur. "Can you beat it? In the middle of a war?"

"Possibly you can get off if you tell them that you are the king."

"Then it would be noised that the king used his position to shirk a sacred obligation."

"Well, you can't have it both ways."

"I knew I could count on you for a sentient word."

"Touching the Prophecy," said Sir Kay.

"Yes?" said Arthur.

"Well, it seems to me that now might be a good time to take a look at it. See if it casts any light on the march of events and all that."

"You want to see it. The Prophecy. The actual document."

"If you think it appropriate, sire. I mean, I suppose now is as good a time as any, don't you think?"

"I'm not managing things to your liking, is that it? I'm losing the war, we have civil strife impending, so best haul out the old Prophecy and check the course. Especially since you really think it doesn't exist, that it's just part of the mumbo-jumbo of kingship, something to generate a little awe among the groundlings—"

"I confess to a measure of simple human curiosity, yes."

"I might let you see a bit of it."

"That would be very good of you, sire."

"Not the whole thing. If I let you see the whole thing, then you'd know as much as I do, wouldn't you."

"Hardly. I am not a king. Thus even were I to *see*, I would not necessarily *discern*, if you take my—"

"True enough. Well, then, I'll let you have a look."

"Excellent."

"On Wednesday, possibly. Wednesday or Thursday."

"Arthur, you're trifling with me."

"Merlin was only seven when he gave utterance. Sitting on a rock. He took a long breath—*in*spiration—and then uttered for seven hours. The Prophecy is divided into seven parts. The part that troubles me the most, at the moment, is Part the Sixth."

IR ROGER de Ibadan talking with the Red Knight, Sir Ironside of the Red Lands.

"Rigidity," said Sir Roger, "is what will bring you down."

"Easy for you to say," said Ironside. "Your peoples have nothing at stake in this war. We have Teutonic hordes ready to come lathering across our borders at any time."

"It's dik-dik-like to let the Party do all the thinking," said Sir Roger. "In my opinion. Individual thought, however cankered or askew, is a necessary precondition to the creative use of existence."

"What's a dik-dik?"

"Small antelope, practically brainless," said Roger. "I don't mean to give offense. But it *pains* me to see grown men and women lying on their backs and baring their throats, as it were."

"The Party embodies the collective wisdom of the people," said the Red Knight. "Also, the Party has access to information the individual doesn't have. I much prefer leaving important decisions to the Party than to a crowd of loonies in Parliament."

"The parliamentary way ensures that the voice of the people is heard."

"But the people, and I do not exclude myself, are for the most part charmingly innocent of public affairs."

"My father used to say the same thing: 'They know more about it than we do, they have information we don't have.' This of a government that was plunging the country into absolute ruin!"

"The Party rescued my country from the most terrible tyranny imaginable," said Ironside. "Not a thing one forgets."

"What about the '37 trials?"

"You weary me," said the Red Knight. "The question is, where is Arthur? Where is Guinevere? Who's running the country?"

"Mordred, from what I hear. I don't know why these people can't read his character. It seems perfectly plain to me."

"Plain as a packsaddle," said the Red Knight. "Even in Russia we know about Mordred."

"People in Russia gossip about the royals?"

"At the kitchen level," said Ironside. "My place has four kitchens. Naturally some of the gossip drifts abovestairs."

"You have servants?"

"Not exactly servants. People who come in to help out now and then."

"How many?"

"Let me see," said Ironside. "We have a steward, a chef, two sous-chefs, several people keeping the accounts—four, I think—a butler, and the maids. Thirteen maids, I believe. And then the grooms and the people who supervise the people in the fields and whatnot. And a vet."

"A dream of beauty, from the black perspective. This is the Revolution?"

"I fought with the Red Army when all of my fellows, or most of them, were with the Whites. The Party remembers."

"You don't seem that old."

"The joy of battle. Keeps you young."

"*Is there* a joy of battle?" asked Sir Roger. "I've experienced it, I suppose, but it is strangely depressing, for joy. I am susceptible to gloom, it's true. I am gloomful, as it were, right this minute."

"I too am gloomy, in these days," said the Red Knight. "It's a combination of the war and my acute historical consciousness."

"Good sir, I think you not half so sorrowful as myself."

"I am more sorrowful than any man I ever met," said the Red Knight, "my acute historical consciousness being widened and deepened by my advanced years. With all respect, your sorrow is but japes to my sorrow."

Then Sir Roger swooned away from sorrow, and woke and swooned again, and every time he woke he swooned anew.

"By Jesu," said the Red Knight, "surely this is the finest sorrow I have ever seen, whether of man or woman, priest or laity. What is it that makes this good knight so full of dolor?"

"It is love," said Sir Roger, awakening. He began to prick at the sleeve of his black doublet with a silver-hilted poniard. "I am mischieved as sorely as Launcelot was the day the lady huntress pierced him with an arrow in the buttock and he could not remove the barb that was six inches deep in him and could not sit a saddle but must needs lie on his belly athwart his poor horse with his legs a-dangling and his great head knocking against the poor beast's side every step of the way to Westminster."

"Stop doing that with the knife," said the Red Knight. "Makes me nervous. Is there, may I ask, some obstacle to the achievement of your hopes? Is the lady cold, or is she, perhaps, enamored of another? Or is it that her husband, saying that she has such an unfortunance, in which case I cannot advise you, as the Central Committee does not approve of liaisons which—"

"Nothing of the sort," said Sir Roger, "yet worse. Love hath laid a bushment for me that hath cause me unawares. The one I love is not an honest woman."

"A woman of bad repute?"

"Oh, excellent repute, within her métier, none better."

"And that métier is?"

"She is a highwayman. Relieved me of a certain sum on the road to Baginton seven days ago. An embarrassingly small sum."

"She subdued a knight in full armor?"

"She had a Sten gun. Her name is Clarice. I

have no idea whether that's real or just a name she uses professionally."

"I take it she's a looker."

"Smashing. She was wearing a sheer blouse."

"I understand."

"It's the mind, you know. Enchants perfectly ordinary things like breasts and makes them seem rare and wonderful."

"Da."

"So you don't think me foolish."

"Not more foolish than any other damned fool."

"I'm pleased."

"Good."

"Still absolutely miserable, you understand."

"Verily."

LYONESSE and Edward on the deck of a tanker, the *Ursala*. Listening to Ezra on the ship's radio.

"The next peace," said Ezra, "won't be made by a pair of kikes, one at each side of the table, or standing behind the stuffed shirts who represent 'em in front of the public. And the basic aim of the peace will not be Versailles's basic aim. Namely, to prepare the next war. That's what Versailles was aimed at, with its daggers and cross-lines, its Skodas, its synthetic states. Its gun factories run with Jew money, run on loans, based on money sweated out of the Aryan peoples, sweated out of the farm laborers and industrial workin' men. The next peace will not be based on international lending. Get that for one. And England will certainly have nothing what bloody ever to say about what its terms are."

"I suppose he's harmless," Edward said. "People can't possibly believe all that rot."

"The pose is a peculiar one," said Lyonesse. "Notice that 'workin' men.' Where'd his *g* get to? If you believe that belly-up-to-the-bar-boys stuff you'll believe anything."

"We'll be reassigned, I imagine," Edward said. "Very likely to different units. Leave first, I imagine. And you have a husband."

"A sort of husband," Lyonesse said.

"That's the end of that, then."

"That's defeatism, that's what that is," Lyonesse said. "Why is everybody all around me so convinced that everything is going to turn out badly? The campaign, the war, you and me—"

"I'm a plasterer," Edward said. "Right at the moment, I'm a fair imitation of an officer and a gentleman, but what I am is a plasterer. And you're a queen, and the king your husband will likely have my head when he finds you."

"Unthank is doubtless in a rage, but he spends most of his time in a rage, nothing new there. I doubt that he's looking very hard."

"I'll probably be arrested the first time I step into a post office. I'll probably be looking at my own photo on the walls, along with those of all the other philanderers."

"Not a post office wall in the world big enough for all of you."

"Never consorted with a queen before."

"How is it?"

"Not too bad. I can see how all those romances and operas and things got written."

"It's rather terrible, being a queen. One has to attend functions. One has to stand there smiling while the local fellow explains how the peat is packaged."

"How *is* the peat packaged?"

"Very skillfully," said Lyonesse, "but the point is, you don't want to know how the peat is packaged and you are pretty damned sure that your good husband, back at the palace, is topping Glenda or one of the other ladies while you are at the inaugural ceremonies for the new peat-packaging facility."

"I see."

"Peat is one of our principal exports, in Gore. The others are bandages of all sizes and pornographic films. My husband takes a personal interest in the film industry."

"A nicely diversified product mix."

"We are prosperous, especially in wartime. But to be a queen, even a country sort of queen, is to know boredom as few humans have known boredom. Chatting up the wounded in the hospitals, for instance. God knows they've suffered and are suffering, but there's just not much to say. 'Hello, where are *you* from? You seem to be lacking a leg, there.' I haven't the gift for it."

"I'll wager you're quite wonderful."

"He even asked me to be in one of them. A film."

"What did you say?"

"I did it. It won a prize at a festival."

"Do you want me to be shocked? I think not."

"It was a scene with another woman. Glenda,

in fact. We had quite a good time. I surprised my-self."

"Can I book it, this film? Local cine club have it?"

"I am trying to make clear to you why I left."

"Not necessary."

"Of course I can *do it,* queening. I have the blood for it."

"Most excellent blood, I'm sure."

"I'll have you made a bishop. You can bless our bed before we jump into it."

"I'd be looking over my shoulder for lightning bolts."

"You'd make a jolly bishop. Stuffing toys into orphans at Christmas. Stuffing—"

"Yes, yes. You have a positive fondness for the illicit."

"The licit hasn't done much for me thus far. How many more days, do you think?"

"Another day and a half, they say."

"Where do we land?"

"They won't tell us. Loose lips sink ships, they say. They say it again and again."

"I wish there were some more of that very good stuff we were drinking back when we were young."

"As a matter of fact," said Edward, "I did a deal with one of the cooks."

"Seize all the brightest toys," said Ezra. "My things are a botch."

"This isn't his usual line," said Lyonesse.

"But I'll write more versus, in the mornings when I feel better. The mad boy 'scapes whipping," said Ezra, "*la gente intanto strillava a tempesta,* nay said the knight I shall never arise till ye grant me mercy."

LOBSTERS," said Arthur.

"What?" said Sir Kay.

"Lobsters are the only thing most people kill with their own hands," said Arthur. "In the modern world."

"Not we," said Sir Kay. "We smite the enemy."

"We are different," said Arthur. "We are professional soldiers. Most people don't even kill chickens. They buy them at the market, neatly wrapped. The encounter between man and lobster remains, in this civilization, the last direct experience of killing something. Write that down."

"Write it down?"

"Yes, it's a thought. I might be able to use it somewhere."

"We have dispatches from London," said Sir Kay. "The queen has departed, leaving Mordred as regent."

"Mordred? What poor judgement."

"I think so too," said Sir Kay. "But you know Guinevere."

"Where is she?" asked Arthur.

"Not sure," said Sir Kay. "In theory, she's trying to find you. But she's not been in touch with anyone since she left."

"Well, she gets restless," said Arthur. "Can't

say that I blame her. It's May; she probably went a-Maying. I get restless too. As a matter of fact, I'm restless right this minute. I think I'll go to Malta. Malta hangs by a thread."

"Malta has been hanging by a thread since December. Hasn't bothered you up to now. Sire."

"Then again, I could go to Morocco."

"We're not fighting in Morocco."

"We may well be, in time," said Arthur. "Perhaps someone should look over the terrain."

"I detect," said Sir Kay, "an evasion of Guinevere."

"Do you now."

"What's that music?"

"Hummel," said Arthur. "The Piano Concerto in A Minor."

"Chandelier music."

"Good Sir Kay, don't be so scornful. I like it."

"It's the wrong kind of music for wartime."

"On the contrary," said Arthur. "Listen to the German radio if you want proper wartime music. I imagine it's driving the people batty."

"Did you hear Haw-Haw this morning?"

"What'd he say?"

"He said that England, as an idea, is through, finished. He said that we are putrefying and that the tides of history were taking the garbage out to sea."

"Water metaphors. I wonder if he was a naval person, over here."

73

"I doubt it. Can the navy be so decayed?"

"Mordred sent me two dozen bottles of excellent claret. It was wanting an occasion."

"Fine gestures butter no parsnips."

"D'you suppose it's poisoned?"

"Sire!" said Sir Kay. "What a notion!"

"Mordred loves no one," said Arthur. "I wonder what he's planning."

"A very dangerous situation," said Sir Kay. "If I may venture an opinion."

"Meseemeth it were best," said Arthur, "that he be replaced by some wise and temperate regent closer to our heart. As soon as possible."

"Gawain?"

"Gawain we need in the field. Similarly, Launcelot. Launcelot has no temperament for governing, in any case. He's far too generous; he'd give away the store in a fortnight. You are the man for the job."

"As you wish," said Sir Kay. "Mordred won't like it."

"Don't suppose he will," Arthur said. "But you, my dear Sir Kay, know how many blue beans make five. I want you in London by tomorrow morning. I'll give Mordred something. Something quite grand. How about Governor-General of the Bahamas?"

"What are the Bahamas?"

"I've never been entirely sure," said Arthur. "Islands, I think. I know only that they're ours and require a governor-general. There's quite a gorgeous uniform, cloak, plumed hat, and a gilded coach drawn by twelve black horses. I saw a photograph of it once. That's the ticket, I should think."

"Won't wash with Mordred," said Sir Kay.

"There are seven hundred islands, I believe," said Arthur. "I'll ask him for a defense survey. The islands are distributed over four thousand four hundred and three square miles. That should keep him occupied."

"You're bloody quick with the figgers," said Sir Kay. "I'm amazed."

"If you're a king," said Arthur, "you have to know a little of this and a little of that. I usually like to be somewhat vague—lost in thought, don'tcha know—but in this case . . ."

"By the way," said Sir Kay. "There's a journalist waiting to see you. He says his name is Pillsbury."

"Is he *The Times?*"

"The *Spectator*," said Sir Kay. "Sorry."

"Must I see him?"

"It's been weeks since you've seen one."

"The last time, I said some things I regretted. Specifically, about Winston."

"This time you'll be more careful."

"I will. Send him in."

HE BLUE Knight cantering along with Sir Roger de Ibadan.

"The Grail is that which will end the war with a victory for the right," said the Blue Knight. "Therefore it follows that it is a weapon of some kind, a superweapon if you will, with which we can chastise and thwart the enemy."

"But what sort of weapon would that be?" asked Sir Roger.

"A bomb, I think," said the Blue Knight. "A really horrible bomb. One more horrible and powerful and despicable than any bomb ever made before. Capable of unparalleled destruction and the most hideous effect on human life."

"Do we really want such a weapon?"

"Well, it's ends and means, isn't it? Do we really want to win the war? Or do we sink into a serflike condition vis-à-vis the enemy? What's the answer?"

"We *must* win the war."

"Cobalt," said the Blue Knight. "I have been reading up on this, and I feel that cobalt is the thing."

"What would you do with it?"

"Well, you'd need to find a detonator. Something that would get the thing started. That's the tricky part."

"Seems far removed from the Grail of old," said Sir Roger.

"New problems demand new solutions."

"Why, if I may ask, are you called the Blue Knight?"

"I am thought to be melancholy."

"On what evidence?"

"Just my temperament, I suppose. I've always been *rather* melancholy, even as a child. Spent a lot of time plucking at the counterpane, as it were. It grew worse as I got older. Also, I published a book. It was called *On the Impossibility of Paradise.*"

"What was the argument?"

"I argued that the idea of a former paradise, which had been lost and might be regained either in this world or in the next, did not square with my experience."

"Personal experience."

"Yes. I wasn't even happy in the womb. The womb, for me, was far from a paradise. I remember distinctly. My mother was a very modern person—*advanced,* don't you know. Fond of Alban Berg, the *Wozzeck* man. Not only was I forced repeatedly to listen to *Wozzeck,* in the womb, but also to *Lulu,* which is even worse, from the fetal point of view. These horrors aside, there was the poetry of Wyndham Lewis, proprietor of *Blast. Blast* was the name of his magazine. Can you imagine calling your magazine *Blast*? Going to crack consciousness wide open, he was. These tidderly-push artists and their conceits—the poetry was of a piece. I had to listen to it. In the womb. In addition, there were certain odd substances entering the bloodstream—do you know what kif is?"

"No idea."

"Better thus. In sum, my womb time was quite hellish, and upon being expelled I found the larger arena not much of an improvement. I don't mean to complain, of course, I'm just trying to suggest—"

"No no," said Sir Roger. "Say on. I suppose we should be doing search-and-destroy, but your remarks are of the greatest interest to me."

"Good of you," said the Blue Knight. "The basic contradiction I located or felt I had located was in terms of dramatic values. Paradise, the Fall, and the return to Paradise—it's not a story. It's too symmetrical. There are no twists. Just Paradise, zip, Fall, zip, and Paradise again, zip. And I had a very strong feeling, an intuition if you will, that even if Paradise were regained it would have music by Milhaud and frescoes by the Italian Futurists."

"But we have something to strive for," said Sir Roger. "It is a great thing, having something to strive for."

"I don't disagree. A Grail, for example."

"And Grail-as-bomb . . . I don't like it."

"Who likes it? But consider the logic. In former times bombing had some military purpose or other—taking out a railyard, smashing the enemy's factories, closing down the docks, that sort of thing. Today, not so. Today, bombing is meant to be a learning experience. For the bombed. Bombing is pedagogy. A citizen with a stick of white phosphorus on his roof begins to think quite seriously about how much longer he wants to continue the war."

"There's that, I suppose."

"There's a race on," said the Blue Knight, "to find the Grail. The other side is hard at it, you may be sure. Myself, I'm partial to cobalt. It's blue."

R. PILLSBURY of the *Spectator,* sire," said Sir Kay. Pillsbury entering, a tall young man in battle dress.

"Sire."

"Mr. Pillsbury."

"Very good of you to see me. I won't take up much of your time, I hope. First, people want to know why you're not in London. I breach no confidences if I say that Mordred is not greatly loved. He makes people uneasy. Why was he made regent at this very difficult moment?"

"There were a number of considerations," Arthur said.

"I'm sure."

"I'm needed in the field. We have plans which of course I can't tell you about. Mordred, whether he's the most likable man in the world or no, is a very competent administrator. The affairs of the kingdom are in excellent hands."

"Mr. Churchill doesn't appear to think so. He was quoted in the press this week as saying that you were an anachronism and that Mordred had a penchant for villainy."

"To whom did he say that?"

"To me. I printed it, and he subsequently denied saying it. Made quite a noise, the whole thing. I'm surprised you haven't seen it."

"We don't exactly devour the newspapers here, Mr. Pillsbury," said Sir Kay. "This is a field headquarters."

"Still, you might want to make a statement, sire. Would you care to comment on the historical question? Do *you* feel you're an anachronism?"

"If Mr. Churchill didn't say it, the question doesn't arise, does it?"

"He said it. I have it in my notes."

"But he says he didn't say it, and I'm quite happy to believe him. Officially, you see, there's nothing to respond to."

"My readers," said Pillsbury, "need, nay, require reassurance as to whether the throne is, in this century, still a viable institution."

"King," said Arthur, "king, king, king. Fundamentally an absurd idea, that one chap has better blood than another chap. Has to do with dogs, dog breeding, really, dogs and horses. Oh, it's no great thing to be a king. On the other hand, I've never *not* been a king, so I've no idea what that's like. Might be quite grand. The pleasure of being inconspicuous, a fudge in the crowd. Can't imagine it.

"Can't imagine what it would be like to be a churl. The country's full of them, yet I have no idea how they think. It's not good for a king to have no idea how people think. By the same token, the people have no idea how *I* think. When I address them, it's in the language of a proclamation, isn't it? And the language of a proclamation is hardly cozy, is it? I could even be witty, and the people would never know. Pity.

"In the same universe of discourse," said Arthur, "the question of leadership, with accompanying subsections, such as statesmanship, generalship, gamesmanship, rabble rousing, and the like. The king's sceptre, the marshal's baton, the conductor's baton, the physician's caduceus, the magician's wand—a stick of some kind, with which one must animate a mass. In your case, Mr. Pillsbury, a pencil. But one must know how to operate the stick, eh? One can't just wave the damned thing around to no purpose. All in the wrist, eh, Mr. Pillsbury?"

"Sire."

"Not unrelated to the above, the king's dealings with those who surround him, to his seneschal, subseneschals, semiseneschals, and seneschals-in-ordinary, and especially the dreadful business of minding the order of rank and precedence among one's vassals. One's vassals are a touchy lot, of that you may be sure. One has secretaries to keep this sort of thing straight, of course, but Lord help you if you seat a baronet whose title is older than the next baronet's wrongly in relation to the sun, that is to say, yourself. Then spending time in the countinghouse is a bore; one could spend eternities in the countinghouse, there's so much to count. Gave it a whirl once, never again. Trusted associates count for me now. Sir Kay counts excellently well—it's one of his skills.

"In this connection, mention must be made of the burden of taxation. I mean the burden on the king. One has to decide some very tricky things. How much a chap's income should one take, morally speaking? Of course one's first inclination is to take it all and be done with it. But studies have shown that if you take every last groat—and I'm not saying it isn't a neat solution and that the individual's not grateful, more or less, for not having to fill out all those tedious forms—you deincentivize him. He stacks arms, to use a military figure, and you lose in the long run. The amount of taxation you can get away with must be nicely judged.

"Not entirely irrelevant in this context is the problem of ermine. Do you know how dear ermine is? One poor devil's taxes for a whole year will hardly buy one ermine tail, and one rich devil's taxes for a whole year won't get you a fully trimmed robe. I wonder that one sees any ermine at all nowadays. Yet if you appear in public on a state occasion with nutria or something trimming your robe, they say that you're skimping on the pomp, the public's bought-and-paid-for pomp. Well, enough about ermine. It's crossed my mind to start up a flock or whatever it is of my own, but one can't do everything, and I've never got around to it.

"Next, one must ensure that the population is properly intoxicated," said Arthur. "Anciently, the cry was *Mead for my men!* Nowadays it's more a matter of seeing to it that there are sufficient licensed premises and that such are adequately supplied by the breweries, that the movement of grain and hops to these from the farmers is unimpeded, and that the flow of revenues to the crown from each of the points at which we take our little nip is not lost to us through inspectatorial ineptitude. I never touch the stuff myself, except perhaps in the heat of battle, when a hogshead of brandy might be broached under especially trying circumstances, but your average walking-about citizen becomes extremely churlish when denied his booze, and it's a thing the ruler does well to keep in view.

"Pursuant to which and outparsable therefrom is the inner turmoil suffered by the king, of which I cannot speak, for if I spoke about it, it would be outer, not inner, and keeping the inner *in* is the very essence of kingship. I can tell you that it makes one spleenful. Whereas most people enjoy a more or less trouble-free spleen, the king's spleen must be vented regularly. This involves cathartics and tubes and pails and things that you don't wish to know about.

"Not wholly distinct from the foregoing is the occluded nature of one's relation to the succession. The succession is not something one wants to think about, but it must be thought about. As you can see, I've evaded the issue so far, the question hasn't come up except in the most general sense. I've been remarkably long-lived, that's a wonder, I don't understand it myself. My life doesn't seem to end.

"Finally and in sum, abstracting and essentializing are what a king does, and I will continue as the humble servant of the British people as long as the great public continues to honor me with this sacred trust. More brandy?"

"The war," said Pillsbury. "What about the war?"

"The situation remains grave, but we anticipate a turning of the tide in the near future."

"That's all?"

"With the help of our valiant allies, the closing of the ring is inevitable."

"Anything more?"

"I think that's enough, Mr. Pillsbury. Very good of you to come."

Withdrawal of the journalist Mr. Pillsbury.

"A feast of blague," said Sir Kay. "And you dodged the Mordred question rather clumsily."

"I think he forgot he asked it."

"So Winston thinks you're an anachronism."

"Ah, well," said Arthur. "I wouldn't be surprised if he was right. God knows I feel like one. I feel old."

"I wonder what he'll write."

"Absolute tosh, of course. Did you like the line about the closing of the ring?"

"First class," said Sir Kay. "The turning of the tide, as well."

"I have a gift for banal metaphors," said Arthur. "I've always had it. Comes naturally, like sweating. What's Winston's? If not the beginning of the end, then the end of the beginning. That's fustian for you."

"He can be quite funny, I think," said Sir Kay. "A master of rhetoric, if nothing else."

"I suppose we'll have to knight him when this is all over. Of course when you knight every Tom, Dick, and Harry in the country, the point of the thing dwindles."

OOD EVENING, fellow English-men," said Lord Haw-Haw. "This is Germany calling. We wonder a bit, if we may be permitted to wonder, about a country whose queen is, to put it mildly, flirting with indiscretion."

"He's on about you again," said Lyonesse.

"It's been days," said Guinevere. "I've been feeling quite neglected."

"No, 'flirting with' is far too kind; Her Most Gracious Majesty has embraced indiscretion, has indeed leapt into indiscretion's lap and licked its hand. Is there a citizen anywhere in the realm who has not been scandalized by the queen's latest escapade? Not content with her flagrant behavior vis-à-vis Launcelot, that noblest of philanderers, we now find her cozying up to a certain Brown Knight, in the vicinity of Pembroke Manor."

"Now how does he know that?" asked the queen.

"It's the spies, mum," said Varley. "They're everywhere, so they say, and they look just like anybody. It's the fifth column."

"A fact, ask any steady man or woman in Pembroke Manor, where this shameful game goes on unrebuked by the just censure of honest folk, as sure as the Common clock is five minutes fast."

"That's true," said Varley. "About the clock."

"And don't think Winnie and his gang aren't having a fine old time on the ratepayers' money. When you poor dears catch on, it's back on the shelf for that crew. In the meantime, the brandy-swilling swine is having a good giggle at your expense. Your blood, fellow Englishmen, and your treasure, going, going, gone. And where is Arthur? Why, sulking in his tent somewhere, looking at himself in the mirror and wondering about the handsome horns which new adorn his brow. Wake up, Englishmen! This war is not your war. If you believe you'll win, you will also believe that featherbeds grow on trees and sneezing increases the size of the female bust. Good evening, Englishmen. Take a look at the Pembroke Common clock!"

"Do you think he's really English?" asked Lyonesse.

"I'm afraid I do. Although I hear a bit of the Irish there too. God knows what doss house they pulled him out of."

"He's horrid, of course, but he *is* funny sometimes."

"I can't hear it, myself. Perhaps I'm paying too much attention to my own miseries. My aloneness."

"But you have Arthur," said Lyonesse. "To say nothing of Launcelot."

"I *have* neither of them, really," said Guinevere. "The one is off God knows where running the war, and the other pops in between dragons, as it were. It's little consolation that they are both so enormously noble and worshipful, when one's bed is empty night after night. But perhaps I'm being crude."

"Blunt. A queen is incapable of crudity."

"So true," said Guinevere, "so true."

"Did you know Unthank?"

"I did, slightly. When he was young. Probably no better then than he is now. But then he had youth; one could imagine fine things of him. Not so much now, I suppose."

"When I met him he was twenty. I imagined fine things of him. The brutish brow then readable in terms of soccer, at which he was most adroit. That maneuver in which they bash the ball with their heads, which always looks so clever on the field. A good head for business, I figgered. This proved to be the case. He's very good with peat; he's increased our peat production by one hundred and twelve percent over the last ten years. Everything else I imagined was wrong."

"Wit you well," said Guinevere, "that it's difficult to be a king. All manner of folk are pulling the king's coat, saying sire, you must do this, and sire, you must see to that, and sire, look you how the other awaits. It would drive me mad; I'd far lever be a queen, although that's no bed of lilies, either."

"Outwardly," said Lyonesse, "a queen is more or less marble. That is what the cheering crowds assume. They are glad to have us but at the same time think of us as pure symbol. We are that, none better at it, but we also have an inner life, concealed from the crowd. In that inner life, we create new myth—myth that will not circulate generally for maybe four or five hundred years but which is yet profound and pregnant."

"Exactly," said Guinevere. "I have oft thought the same myself but have never been able to phrase it so neatly and, may I say, comprehensively."

"The queenly state," said Lyonesse, "not given to the mult, is a perilous one in that all actions of the queen-person, including lack of actions, are myth-creating whether we like it or not. The press has much to do with this, of course, as your own experience with the Launcelot thing must have persuaded you."

"You cannot imagine how horrible they are," said Guinevere. "One finds them going through one's trash, trying to find something incriminating."

"I don't have to imagine," Lyonesse said. "I once found one under the bed, when I was married to Unthank. Lad from the *Morning Telegraph*. I had had a friend home to tea, a male friend, as it happened, and we were just lying down for a nap, after tea, when Cecil spotted the bugger's foot. It was sticking out. Under the bed. Cecil reached for his sword, and had I not dissuaded him, we would have had blood on the carpet. As it was, we had catastasis."

"What is catastasis?"

"The intensified action directly preceding the catastrophe. In this case, a bash in the nose."

"And this young man with whom you're presently involved—not Cecil, I take it."

"Not Cecil. His name is Edward, and he is a plasterer. Essentially. At the moment, a first lieutenant. He was just promoted."

"You can't marry him, of course. Because of his blood. His blood and his money. He hasn't near enough of either."

"I had in mind living in sin, as they say. For a time. A lovely time, with lots of bed and cognac and perhaps only three servants, and I'd make shepherd's pie and things to save money."

"I doubt that you'd be able to stick it for very long," said Guinevere. "Shepherd's pie requires a special temperament. To eat it, I mean, more than once a year or so."

"But something has happened," said Lyonesse.

I'VE QUITE lost my way," said Launcelot.

"Lost in a dark wood," Sir Roger agreed. "With every possibility of misadventure."

"The trees assume fearful shapes, because it is so dark. That one there resembles nothing so much as a flaming sword. By the way, when I told you earlier that I'd never met a Red, I was forgetting Sir Ironside of the Red Lands. Because he is a knight, I have trouble thinking of him as a Red."

"I was pleased to make his acquaintance," said Sir Roger. "What's that over there?"

"It has the character of a golden cup or chalice," said Launcelot. "But I'm sure it's just a tree."

"Haw-Haw is saying that the Americans are in Hitler's pocket and intend to sit out the war," Sir Roger said. "Wonder if there's any truth in it."

"I doubt it," Launcelot said. "Although how he knew that Guinevere's ablutions habitually include the use of Crabtree's Strawberry Bath Beans is beyond me."

"He was on the mark, in that instance."

"I believe so."

"They say Arthur has made Sir Kay regent and that Sir Kay is going to London to take over the government."

"Sir Kay is an excellent man but far too easy-going for an assignment of that kind, in my opinion."

"I wonder Arthur didn't send you."

"He thinks I have no talent for diplomacy. It's not true. I remember once when Rience, at that time King of North Wales and Ireland, sent a messenger to Arthur demanding that he flay off his beard and send it to him as a tribute. This Rience was bedecking a mantle with kings' beards and had eleven kings' beards as purfles on his mantle already, and one place on the mantle lacked a purfle, and he required Arthur's beard for that place."

"I'll wager he got no worship of Arthur."

"Arthur was ready to go to war over the matter, but I found a goat, a rather elegant black-bearded goat, and flayed off his beard and sent it to the egregious Rience in a crystal casket, and he put it on his mantle and told everyone that it was Arthur's beard. After he'd had the pleasure of boasting about it for several weeks, we leaked the story to one of the sillier newspapers, *News of the World* I think it was. Made page one."

"Look at that," said Roger. "A tree which has shaped itself into a semblance of a trombone."

"Thought I heard music," said Launcelot, "but I see no player, and the thing can hardly play itself."

"And remark that one," Roger said, "a self-stirring caldron, from which delicious smells emanate."

"I smell fennel," Launcelot said. "That reminds me, I should tell you I have discovered a specific for maims. You take salt, good-quality river mud, and bee urine, and slather it on the maim and hold it there for two days. Works like a charm. Gathering the bee urine is a bit of a bore."

"This forest simply teems with interesting iconography," said Roger. "There the trees limn a great chessboard, and the pieces moving by themselves, only they are the same color, silver, on both sides of the board—"

"If you look quickly to your right, you'll see a flying red-and-white horse, the kind the Lady of the Lake likes to send to people who are wanting a horse."

"And now a small castle, wrought of shining brass, which revolves, so that you cannot get in at the door!"

"Well," Launcelot said, "I see sunlight up ahead."

"Amazing place," said Roger. "Of the highest anthropological interest. Do you think one would be able to find it again?"

"Of course not," said Launcelot. "It's an absolute rule, concerning such places, that they can never be found twice. As with fairy gold or Merlin's burial place. Many folk have found Merlin's grave once, usually in Scotland somewhere, but no one has ever found it twice, and indeed, no sensible man would wish to."

"One doesn't want the search to end."

"Just so. For example, I've been thinking about getting a new wristwatch. For the last ten years. Everywhere I travel, I look at wristwatches in shop windows. Seen a great many splendid wristwatches. Were I to actually *buy* a new wristwatch, one of my most pleasant diversions would be denied me."

"One could apply the same logic to wives."

"Don't be shrewd," said Launcelot. " 'Tis unbecoming in a good and worshipful knight."

"Did you see the hanged man? Back there?"

"I did. I wasn't going to mention it."

"Hanged by the foot."

"Yet still alive, by the look of him."

"Methinks he is a murderer or other miscreant."

"Hanging is usually a sign of societal disapproval," said Launcelot, "but let us go back and ask him what he has done."

The knights approached the upside-down man, and Sir Roger prodded him with the tip of his spear.

"Good day," he said. "You seem to be faring poorly, here under the Tree of Knowledge. Is there a reason for it?"

"Alas," said the Hanged Man, "I am sorely abused by those who mislike my politics."

"What arguments produce so forceful a rebuttal?"

"I am a Deviationist," said the Hanged Man,

95

"one of those who believe that only Deviation can redeem the ills of the world."

"A Deviationist," said Sir Roger. "That takes the gilt off the gingerbread, doesn't it?"

"Takes the gilt off the gingerbread," said Launcelot, "that's quite colorful. Something they say in Dahomey?"

"My own invention," said Sir Roger. "Might I ask what a Deviationist does?"

"Deviates," said the Hanged Man, "from whatever is a-doing. Whatever the common herd is up to, we go athwart it, on principle. Naturally this does not make us loved."

"I think this chap is a locus of ill luck," said Launcelot. "We'd best be off and leave him to the crows."

"No no," said Sir Roger. "We'll never learn anything that way. His is an interesting notion. Methinks we tarry until we get the hang of it, as it were."

"I could discourse perhaps more sweetly," said the man, "were you to cut me down."

"We can't do that," said Sir Roger. "It's interfering with due process. I assume there was due process."

"Mobs of due process," said the Hanged Man, "every hand a registered voter."

"Must be some paperwork about," Sir Roger said, looking everywhere. "The sentence, the appeal, the denial on review, the—"

Launcelot wrapped his left arm around the man and cut the rope.

"Gramercy," said the Hanged Man, rubbing his leg. "My principles were fading fast. We Deviationists are of two kinds," he began, "Deviationists and True Deviationists."

"I suspect this will be rather a long disquisition," said Sir Roger.

"Look you," said Launcelot, "there's something written on the hanged chap's leg."

"A rope burn, perhaps."

"Appears to be a mathematical formula of some sort."

"Perhaps I'd better copy it. Might be important."

"Oh, I doubt it. He's hardly the sort of person who'd have something important written on his leg."

"Be that as it may," said the Black Knight, and began copying.

O," MORDRED said.

"Do I understand you to say 'no'?"

"Your hearing, good Sir Kay, is adequate to the occasion. The answer is no."

"Then we'll have to mount a campaign against you."

"Actually, launching military operations is now my prerogative. Legally, I am the chief officer of the government, thanks to the queen's famous lightness of mind. I admit that the people love Arthur and will doubtless follow him. I have, however, military units loyal to me, and a not small number of people see in me an alternative to the great king. Should Arthur wish to level London, that is possible."

"London suffers grievously from the bombing. Arthur would not wish it more destruction."

"So I had imagined."

"It's a bit of a stalemate, then."

"Furthermore, I must tell you that I have caused Westminster Abbey, the Houses of Parliament, the British Museum, the Victoria and Albert, and certain other notable buildings to be mined. I may or may not have excepted the palace. We told the workmen they were digging shelters. If Arthur chooses, he can produce a not inconsiderable amount of notable rubble at a word."

"This is all quite mad."

"It's a fantasy," said Mordred. "Mine. I've entertained myself with it since I was a boy."

"Unspeakably vile. What do you hope to achieve?"

"I want Arthur to get himself killed. Gloriously, if possible."

"But he's your father."

"As much a father to me as a sickle to a stand of wheat. I will not bore you with a recounting of his shortcomings. It is enough that you know I hold myself fatherless. You will so inform him."

"He's not likely to oblige you."

"I suppose not. Still, I've put him on the edge of the cliff. Maybe the wind—"

"But what, if I may put it this way, do you think you represent? Leadership is always the embodiment of a principle of some sort, and I can't make out yours."

"An antidote to kingliness, perhaps."

IR PERCY Plangent has writ a new opera attacking Arthur!"

"It is called *The Grail,* and in it the Grail is a bomb that will make everyone happy forever!"

"A bomb that will make everyone happy forever! Is this the same bomb that the Blue Knight was speaking of, some time ago?"

"In the opera the device does not use cobalt, as the Blue Knight projected, but bold euphonium!"

"What is euphonium?"

"It's a compound of europium and eurekium. In Act One, it is discovered. In Act Two, it is refined. In Act Three, it explodes!"

"In the first act, everybody denounces Arthur for not having a wonderful bomb like this. In the second act, everybody decides that something must be done. In the third act, the bomb goes off!"

"A powerful parable of political praxis!"

"Precisely! The bomb is a metaphor for the unhappiness of those groaning under the yoke!"

"Who is groaning under the yoke?"

"The folk are groaning under the yoke!"

"And is the music modern?"

"Wondrous modern! Only nineteen notes are used, but these are bullied so relentlessly, configured and reconfigured with such incessantness, that the orchestra must be replaced between each act!"

"Clarice, the highwayman, is singing the leading female role!"

"Her talents are many and various! She is a living, breathing provocation!"

"She sings with one breast exposed! A large and shapely one, Roman in character!"

"In that it suggests both succor and revolution!"

"Sir Roger sits, night after night, in the first row of the balcony, his jaw agape!"

"His heart is cruelly torn! His loyalty to Arthur—"

"Is there fighting in the stalls?"

"And hullabaloo in the bars! Many a cracked skull attests the brains enflamed and livers ruffled!"

"Not till Arthur abdicates will riot cease its flow!"

"And that he will never! Sir Kay attempted to halt a performance and had his person all besmeared with anchovies and sputter!"

"It must be true, then, what they say!"

"What do they say?"

"They say that when the mode of the music changes, the form and shape of the state changes!"

"A most pernicious thought! It likes me ill!"

"Things yet to come will make us sadder still!"

T THE Café Balalaika, Launcelot and Guinevere drinking coffee.

"All these people who don't know who we are!"

"Anonymity," said Launcelot, "is something I have always cherished."

"This place is *très gai*. Speaking of that, I am afraid that the conductor of the Royal Philharmonic must be let go."

"Why?"

"His programming. He'll perform nothing but requiems. Fauré, Berlioz, Mozart, Verdi, Dvořák, Hindemith . . ."

"In time of war, not such a bad thing."

". . . over and over. I take his point, but the audiences deserve something a bit more inspiriting, wouldn't you say? Bit of jollity in there somewhere? You, of course, would find his concerts much to your taste. The Dies Irae side of you."

"I am hardly fit for human society, that's true."

"*Wonderfully* severe," Guinevere said. "You clatter in your sleep, you know. Wonderfully. Myself, I've having an attack of breathlessness."

Launcelot reaching for her.

"Not here."

"I am a caitiff fellow," he said, "that I can bring no joy to my love."

"The fault is mine, I promise you. I am as empty as an oyster shell. When you're away, I invent a self, make up a Guinevere, and live that Guinevere. But on those infrequent occasions when you are with me, that Guinevere takes herself off, and I'm left with . . . a breathlessness, I suppose."

Launcelot hanging his head.

"I am a foul unworshipful caitiff," he said, "and I must go away now to pray your forgiveness."

"You must *go away* to pray my forgiveness?"

"There is a little hut where I do penance. In Cardiganshire. Much like a lazar-cote. I sit in steam and flagellate myself. I will repair thither straightaway."

"A wonderful idea," said Guinevere. "I'll go with you."

"You must not. You'll be seeing Arthur shortly."

"I have not seen him these many months. I'm told he's aged."

"Arthur is eternal," said Launcelot. "You might as well say of a stone that the stone has aged."

"His behavior toward me exhibits, at times, a stoniness. But I shouldn't complain. He has been, for all these years, a good husband. After his own definition."

A waiter approaching with a long flower box, ecru in color.

"You've got me flowers. How dear of you."

"I haven't," said Launcelot. "Although I clearly should have."

"It's addressed to the gentleman," said the waiter.

Launcelot opening the box.

"What is it?"

"It's my mace, my second-best mace. I left it in the men's room at the Lamb and Flag some time ago. Someone's returned it."

"There's a message."

He opened the envelope.

"Not a message, a scribble. Appears to be a mathematical formula of some sort." He stuck the paper in his doublet. "I'm very glad to have this back, in any case. Never expected to see it again."

"Does it have a name?"

"I call it Stream-of-Anguish."

"Very warlike. Most intimidating."

"I spend my whole life *hacking* at things," Launcelot said. "Is this the best way to exist in the world?"

"At least your worship is conceded by everyone. In my case, everyone thinks I am merely this or merely that—merely beautiful, usually. They say I get everything I want by being beautiful."

"I, by hacking."

"They say I haven't got a brain in my head. They say that I am a terrible woman and will be the ruination of the kingdom."

"Hacking away, day in and day out; get a thing properly hacked and there's the next thing, begging for hacking. . . ."

"They say they say they say . . ."

"Shouldness is being flouted here," said Launcelot. "Shouldness is perhaps self-explanatory, but I have never seen it adequately dealt with, either in print or in the lecture hall. When that huntress got me in the bum with an arrow, it was an offense to shouldness. It shouldn't have gone that way. I told the story to Sir Roger, and now he never tires of telling it, tells it to everyone who comes down the pike. That a knight of the Table Round could be pierced in that way by a female has a significance quite apart from the ludicrous. It's in the realm of those things which *should not happen*—a category which holds much philosophical interest, as anyone who has ever looked into anomaletics will recognize. The insult to my dignity was not nearly so grave as the insult to shouldness."

"Quite," said Guinevere.

"Our love is, similarly, an affront to shouldness —first to conventional morality and then to unconventional morality in that it's so damned difficult to pursue, with journalists coming out of the woodwork and Arthur being impossibly noble about the whole thing and all that. The *should* of love is that something is possible, at least."

"Right," said the queen.

"I'm pleased that you understand me so well," said the knight. "I expected nothing less. The war is of course another example."

"Of course," said the queen. "Should we go back to my place now?"

HERE ARE too many Negroes in Britain," said Haw-Haw. "Your in-migration from Egypt, India, the Caribbean, and God knows where is ruining the country. Too many boongs in Albion, white people. You will lose the war."

"Vicious little devil, isn't he," said Arthur.

"He has quite a tongue," Launcelot said. "Tell me, have you ever met a truly black knight?"

"You mean black-black?"

"Yes."

"Can't say that I have."

"I have met one," Launcelot said, "and he is a rare fellow indeed. From Africa. Glittering with accomplishment. I will bring him to you so that you may hold converse with him, if you like."

"Launcelot, you're evading the issue."

"Which?"

"The war. It's going badly. All our commanders in the field are performing miracles, but it's still going badly."

"The tide will turn."

"No, it won't," said Arthur. "It's Winston. He's laboring under the impression he's running things. Have you seen the war room he's dug for himself under Whitehall?"

"I have not."

"Damnedest thing I ever saw. He's got map rooms and telex rooms and decoding rooms and *en*coding rooms and God knows what all. And a suitably ascetic bedroom for those times when the burden of waging war constrains him to spend the night. An army blanket on the bed. The place goes on for miles. After the war, the whole thing will be a Winston Museum, mark my words. The red telephone, the green telephone, the blue telephone—"

"He's not really a military feller," Launcelot said. "Not as we conceive such. Although I suppose the navy is a military force, of a kind. He's lost us a couple of battleships, I hear."

"The *Prince of Wales* and the *Repulse*," said Arthur. "And there are two more sunk that nobody knows about yet. The Italians got them in the harbor. Frogmen."

"Sweet Jesu."

"Who is this Brown Knight Haw-Haw has been raving about?"

"I doubt there's any such person. I asked Guinevere about it point-blank, and she replied, 'Fiddle.' I am as ready to be jealous as any man, but there are conjectures 'tis better not to entertain. What Tennyson calls 'The war of Time against the soul of man' proceeds by just such imaginings."

"True. I congratulate you, by the way, on the capture of that armored battalion in Norway."

"It was only a battalion."

"It was a marvel. A whole battalion taken by one man! Are there any decorations you don't already have?"

"I think not."

"We'll create a new one, then. Something with a rose . . ."

WALTER the Penniless addressing the multitude.

"And if I say to my flock, 'Hither!' it flocketh hither, and if I say to it 'Thither!' it flocketh thither, for know that I have sought always, I have endeavored to the best of my ability, to shepherd my flock in the directions meseemeth best, even though another might counsel quite otherwise, or a hundred others. Seeking, then, to place yourself with regard to the flock, know that you are either within the flock or outside of the flock, as the lamb which strayeth from the flock is outside of the flock, and in mortal danger of the wolf, that seeketh those which falleth away from the flock. And just as the wolf seeketh he who hath fallen away from the flock, the better to engorge him and tear his flesh, so too the miscreant members of the Round Table do batten upon the flesh and treasure of England, against the Divine Will, no matter how they mouth 'Sweet Jesu' and 'Jesu mercy' and 'Jesu deliver me' and 'Jesu be your speed' and suchlike, it is their own worship and pelf they cultivate, to the affront of common folk who are groaning in their shires and hamlets and in their hutments and bawdy burghs. Know you that in my own conduct I have never been influenced from any regard of mine own inter-

III

est or honor, or desire to appear wiser than others or superior to them or answering to anything but a careful, strict, and tender regard to the will of Our Blessed Lord, learned by me after a long, diligent, impartial, and prayerful inquiry. And the Lord saith that it is the pomp and orgulity of these that call themselves 'true knights' and 'the fellowship' that grindeth the faces of the poor and tax every man beyond endurance and take unto themselves every good thing that is the fruit of the honest man's labor and the honest woman's striving. And that they will be England's ruin and that it is the duty of every honest man and woman to bring them low and smash them and drag them in the dirt. And if you heed me not then I shall show you weeping and gnashing of teeth, teeth gnashed to pumice and weeps a mile high, little bits of tooth littering the fair countryside and so many weeps wept that it were like unto—"

"I do love a good tonguelashing," said the Yellow Knight. "Makes me want to go out and slice some fellow's liver off."

"Invigorating," the Blue Knight said. "Tonic."

"I agree," said the Hanged Man.

F WE could build a wall," said Arthur, "a great wall around everything we hold dear, and defend that wall, to the death of course, with everything we hold dear inside it, and everything we do not hold dear outside it—"

"It's been tried," said Sir Roger. "The French tried it with the Maginot Line—little good it did them—and then the Chinese, famously—"

"Siege mentality," said Arthur. "I know it's wrong from a military point of view, but how comforting, how luxurious, looking over the plans with the engineers, the walls six feet—no, eight feet— no, twelve feet thick. Just thinking of the thickness and height of the walls is a great pleasure, designing the strong points, laying out fields of fire—"

"I understand they bombed Coventry again last night."

"And Birmingham, and Manchester, and Mordred threatening to blow up everything the Nazis miss—"

"The cathedral was quite smashed up, they say."

"I am thinking of cutting my throat," said Arthur. "I know that this is not a course of action open to kings."

"It's not something that will make your name

resound in song and story," said Sir Roger. "On the other hand, perhaps we concern ourselves overmuch with the good opinion of posterity. Our Benin kings are quite contemptuous of it. They say: I do as I please, and if the folk do not like it, let them kill me if they can."

"Someone will kill me, I do not doubt it," said Arthur. "I don't even mind waiting for the fatal thrust. It's only that having one of the choices available to ordinary men barred to me rankles. Of course everything rankles these days. Don't you find that?"

"I haven't your burdens, sire. My days are tolerably pleasant, except for being in love, which is, as I'm sure you know, torment of the most exquisite sort."

"Yes, tell me about it," said Arthur. "Amazing to hear of black people being in love. No offense, mind you. It's quite reasonable, when one thinks about it."

"Many of the emotions generally attributed to the human species are found in black people," said Sir Roger. "In this particular case, there is a problem. The lady is not entirely suitable."

"How not?"

"She exists outside the law. The short form is, she's a thief."

"A thief! How refreshing. Technically, I should cut her hands off."

"She hasn't been apprehended. She remains at large. And far from me."

"On the other hand, I could pardon her, if you wish."

"That would be most gracious of your majesty. But I doubt that she would want it. She likes being a thief."

"What's her name?"

"Clarice."

"There's an old adage that says before you do a favor for someone, make sure he's not a madman. You're not a madman, are you?"

"Not to my knowledge."

"Good. Then let's do this: I'll have her arrested and remanded into your custody. You can discuss the attractions of a life of crime versus those of a royal pardon at your leisure. Possibly there'd be a chance to press your suit, as the expression runs."

"Your majesty is too kind."

"To return to our earlier theme," Arthur said, "I understand that I have to be killed by something. I would prefer that it be music."

HAT DO you think about the war? About the wind? About chivalry? About sex between young persons?" asked Sir Roger.

"A nasty business," said Clarice. "Mostly a struggle for possession of one's own clothes, as I remember. Why do you ask?"

"I'm trying to find out what you think about things," said Sir Roger, "so that if we, for example, marry—"

"A nasty business," Clarice said. "I once knew a woman who was married, married to a jongleur. He wandered, morning noon and night. Jongled his way into many a bed. She claimed he had a thirteen-inch cock. Little good it did her."

"What do you think about food?" asked Sir Roger. "About real estate? About the cross-channel tunnel? About the C. of E.? About people who are black?"

"I think about soup a great deal," she said. "Some of my widest and deepest thoughts are about soup. When I was a child, there was never enough soup. That is why, I suppose, I became a highwayman. Now I have vats of soup, vats and vats. Chicken soup, barley soup, cream of mushroom, lobster bisque—"

"What do you think about going away? With me? Would you like to see Africa? I have a rather splendid place just outside Ibadan, and another near Lagos, on the water—that's the Gulf of Guinea—"

"Going away," Clarice said, "that's an idea. One thing I like about men is that they have ideas, grand impossible ideas, ideas like *going away*—"

"Not impossible. Very possible."

"Wonderful sweeping soul-replenishing ideas that sound good for about five minutes. Until you think about them. I have no prejudice, by the way. I consider black people fully as foolish as white people. Good for thieving from and for little else."

"Give it up," said Sir Roger. "The king will pardon you if I make myself responsible for your good behavior. Then—"

"*Mon cul,*" she said. "Do I look demented? Might as well hand you a leash."

"You'd prefer a noose?"

"They'd have to catch me first, wouldn't they? And they never will."

"Alas," said Sir Roger, "I had hoped to persuade you. I'm not doing a very good job of it."

"You're a fine man," said Clarice, "but it's soup I want, thank you very much."

"The ten pounds six you took from me on the road to Baginton—"

"What about it?"

"Now that we are in a more civil relationship—"

"Business is business," said Clarice, "sentiment is something else. Your ten pounds went right into the market. What I call the stock pot. 'Tis simmering thriftily there even as we speak."

"I cannot live without you."

"You've lived without me perfectly well up to this date."

"Imperfectly and not well."

"Life has many sad strokes left to give you, handsome fellow. If only you were a parsnip . . . I've had quite a letch for parsnips, these last few days."

WHERE IS Puerto Rico?" asked Arthur.

"It's in Venezuela," said Sir Kay. "The northern part."

"Well, it's entered the war, on our side," said Arthur. "That's gratifying. Sir Richard Hubrace is dead. Mysteriously murdered."

"Is that *The Times?*"

"The *Chronicle*. Sir Richard had little bits of caviar between his teeth. Not the best kind. Icelandic."

"Amazing what one discovers about people," said Sir Kay. "I remember him as very free with his money. One wouldn't think he'd have less than Beluga."

"The Nazis have taken Paris. Hitler has visited the tomb of Napoleon."

"Those two have much to say to each other."

"No no no. The one is vermin compared to the other."

"True, but the totalizing impulse. Common to them both. The kind that can't stop at a reasonable stopping point."

"It's Mussolini I regret. He's temporized every step of the way. Lain back hoping to pick up the crumbs. Had to be dragged into the war. Diplomacy might have kept him safely out of it—his or ours. Both were inadequate."

"Any other notable deaths?"

"Sir Bully Kent, the art dealer. Seventy-seven."

"How much did he get?"

"One, two, three columns. Starts on page one but below the fold, of course."

"The newspapers," said Sir Kay, "are our Les Invalides."

"Ninety-four inches," Arthur said, putting away his pocket rule, "and a two-column photo of that villa he had outside Florence."

"Not too bad."

"Tell me something," Arthur said. "Why have I lived so long?"

"God's grace, Merlin's magic, adroitness in battle, sturdy red and white corpuscles, a great heart— What can I say?"

"You don't think it's been a bit . . . protracted? My life?"

"It's run on a few centuries beyond the normal span, that's true. But there are exceptional individuals in all periods of history. Remember Methuselah."

"Ugh! Always struck me as a chap who'd seriously overstayed his welcome."

"Not at all," said Sir Kay. "Quite highly regarded in his own culture, I believe. Of course his culture is not our culture. We have more of a youth culture, modernly. Youth is the thing. Now you take that Sir Roger. A handsome man and positively bursting with youth and vitality. That's the beau ideal today. Age is less a value per se."

"I dreamed last night that I was in bed with a young woman," said Arthur. "I had seen her on the street and she had looked at me, and then looked again. A second look. Then we were in bed together. Then she got up and left, because I was married. She was scrupulous about that, quite properly so. I awoke thinking about the second look. I was grateful for it."

"You are the king," said Sir Kay. "All eyes upon you."

"I felt she didn't know that. That it was *myself,* in some way, that had fetched her."

"What a fine feeling," said Sir Kay. "Luxuriate."

"Then I had another dream, in which I was in bed with a bear. Big hairy bear, male. Much less satisfactory."

"You seem to be dreaming a great deal in these days."

"I do, don't I? The bear was a king too. Spoke Latin and smelled bad."

"What did he say?"

"My Latin is not the best, but I *think* he said something to the effect that 'when there are bears on the boulevards, then the state is tottering.' "

"What is the Latin?"

"Beyond me. *Are* there bears on the boulevards, do you think?"

"None have been reported as yet. But dreams are always prophetic."

"And you, dear Sir Kay. What do you dream?"

"Well, we've been on short rations around here, as you know. Myself, I dream of cheese. Toasted, mostly."

"T IS the king!"

"Why is he solitary upon this brownish sullen plain, where every prospect vexes?"

"Methinks he's taking thought!"

"He's frowning a great frown!"

"His visage is stark with pain!"

"He is wearing a simple white lawn shirt with black trousers!"

"His noble locks, now gray, fall about his shoulders in a fullish manner!"

"He smites himself across the brow with his right hand!"

"He is remembering!"

"Remembering what?"

"His sins!"

"A grand life means grand sins!"

"What, think you, was the grandest?"

"I would say trying to have Mordred killed when Mordred was a child!"

"Yes, that was pretty close to unacceptable!"

"Now he's putting something together!"

"What is it?"

"It appears to be a fishing rod!"

"But there are no fish here!"

"And no water, either!"

"Still, he sits, the king sits!"

"He's fishing!"

"He's fishing as hard as he can!"

"They say it's a sign of senility, fishing under such conditions!"

"It doesn't make much sense to me!"

"A clear indication of a weakening grasp of reality, they say!"

"I do in part believe it! He appears to have hooked something!"

"He strains against the rod! He is pulling an object from the bowels of the earth!"

"Sweet Jesu mercy, it's a fish!"

"Not only a fish but a good fish, a large fish, a plump fish, a ripe and bouncing fish!"

"Certes, this is a true wonder that we see here!"

"It is passing great and marvelous!"

"This puts paid to all talk of the king's inadequacy!"

"He is as able as ever he was!"

"It is a miracle of the rarest order!"

"Let us hurry to the towns and cities to amplify the deed to every man and woman in those shires!"

"With the best will in the world!"

OOD thinking," Clarice said to Lyonesse. "Have the booby's baby, by all means. After the war you can be Mrs. Plasterer. You don't know what these chaps look like when they get out of uniform. Well, of course you do, but you know what I mean. When the wartime atmosphere goes away. And with a brat squalling in the background—"

"It's not a thing queens do. I mean, marry a commoner. When a king gives up the throne for the woman he loves, he becomes a duke, usually. A queen becomes—what?"

"I see a bed-sitter somewhere," said Clarice. "East Turnipseed."

"I do love Edward. I love my life, my recent life. My old life in Gore, playing at Lady Nevershit, was an abomination. And I'm rather curious about the baby."

"I suppose I could get you started in crime & punishment," said Clarice. "On the crime side of the thing, of course. Armored cars, I think. Have you any experience of armored cars? Poor pregnant woman standing by the side of the road weeping buckets. Tattered shawl over bent head, rotten boots enterribled by our own skilled artisans, toil-worn hands clasped over big belly, not actually toil-worn, but we slather some toil glop on them. . . . The armored car skids to a stop, the guard-person descends, leaving his door open, contrary to what the manual instructs, you pop out a Thompson—"

"What's a Thompson?"

"All in good time," said Clarice. "What am I going to do about the member for Ibadan?"

"How do you feel about him?"

"I like him. He'd never go for C & P, he's far too proper. *Very* likely to get himself killed in the war; statistically, those worshipful knights go like vodka at a tea party. You understand the problem: there's nothing to *do* with him. River pirate is a thing I've never tried; I believe Africa has some mighty rivers—"

"Edward is quite a decent sort, overall."

"A prince, if you decide to keep him."

"I think I will."

"I'll retire, I suppose. Maybe get into some-thing white-collar, something Roger won't notice. Boosting tiny thises and thats from museums, Courbets and things. Your average Courbet isn't all that big. Bite-size, as it were."

"But the war—"

"The war is a question. I don't know the an-swer."

AUNCELOT, Arthur, Sir Kay, the Blue Knight, and Sir Roger de Ibadan in conference.

"These three equations, taken together, will enable us to build a bomb more powerful than any the world has ever known," said Sir Roger. "When Launcelot showed me all three, I recognized instantly that they were either alchemical transmutations of the most important kind or the culmination of some Scandinavian work in atomic fission I've been following."

"Or both," said the Blue Knight.

"Or both," Sir Roger agreed. "Either way, it's the Grail you chaps have been seeking. The big boom."

"Amazing that a black man knows that much physics," said Arthur. "I mean no offense, Sir Roger. You are such a wise and accomplished knight that I have trouble thinking of you as a black person sometimes."

"We have a perfectly good university in my country," said Sir Roger, "although the physics department could be stronger, I feel."

"The point is," said the Blue Knight, "someone has given Launcelot the key to the future."

"Certainly cooks Mordred's goose," said Launcelot. "He'll have to capitulate on the mere mention of the bomb."

"How long will it take to build one, do you think?" asked Arthur.

"Matter of months," said the Blue Knight, "putting the science boffins to work triple shifts. But where did the notes come from? Who put the slips in Launcelot's Girl Guide cookie box and so on?"

"Very probably Merlin," said Arthur. "It has his stamp. The kind of show he delights in, the step-by-step unveiling . . ."

"But Merlin's dead."

"In a sense," said Arthur. "With Merlin there's no certainty."

"We can use this to do more than solve the Mordred problem," said Sir Kay. "It will knock out Germany and Italy as well."

"Would we even have to use it?" asked the Blue Knight. "If we merely notified them we had it, that seems to me—"

"Perhaps a demonstration," said Sir Kay. "Do Essen or Kiel or one of the smaller cities."

"You understand," said Sir Roger, "that once you let go of this, the city is gone. Totally. According to my rough calculations, everything within ten miles or so of the point of impact goes. And you could increase the effect by timing the device to go off in the air, fifty or a hundred feet from the ground."

"Isn't that a bit bloodthirsty?"

"That's the business we're in, at the moment."

Arthur took the three slips of paper and tore them to bits.

"We won't do it," he said. "I cannot allow it. It's not the way *we* wage war."

"If we don't," said Sir Kay, "you may be sure that someone else will. Most likely the enemy."

"That may be," said Arthur. "Still, we won't. The essence of our calling is right behavior, and this false Grail is not a knightly weapon. I have spoken."

"Why, Arthur!" exclaimed Launcelot. "That's astonishing. Not doing a thing of this magnitude? I don't think there's been a king in the history of the world who's *not done something* on this scale."

"It's a skill I've been working on for a long time," Arthur said. "I call it negative capability."

"It quite restores my faith in shouldness," Launcelot said.

"But I must tell you that not doing this will have the gravest consequences for ourselves," Arthur said. "In ways I see only dimly. For the Table Round as an institution, and for—"

"Restores my faith in shouldness and sets a noble example for all the world," Launcelot said. "Arthur, I am wondrous proud of you, as are all these gentlemen."

"Long live the king!" all exclaimed, and tears brast from their eyen, and they swooned away to the ground.

'M QUITE angry at her," said Edward, "about the baby, I mean. Surely even queens know how to manage such things?"

"The latest is a philtre that gives one the first trimester to consider the matter," said Sir Roger. "If, after taking thought, reading the omens, and holding the appropriate discussions with other interested parties, the woman decides against it, she takes a second philtre, chemically keyed to the first. A third philtre, which can be added after six point five additional days, allows her to change her mind, once. I read about it. In the *Journal of Reproductive Technology*."

"You read the damnedest things," Edward said. "The point is that she's enfeebled us by a third, as an economic unit. Made the feeble even feebler. *I* can do romantic poverty, *she* might even enjoy it for a time—the stub of a candle guttering in the wine bottle, the landlord battering at the door for the rent money. But with a kid, it'll be straight to Harrods for all the necessaries, sure as my name is Edward Musgrove."

"A fine name," said Sir Roger, "beloved of Jane Austen, among others. Lyonesse and Clarice have been thick as thieves lately, no pun intended."

"I wonder what they're talking about."

"Ourselves, I should hope," said Sir Roger.

131

"But what exactly are they saying? Is Lyonesse favorably disposed toward me, do you think? I hate to ask so bluntly, but in this case—"

"Lyonesse thinks you handsome as the dawn," said Edward. "Great fun listening to her discourse on that point, as you may imagine. She has some doubts about Africa. A most irrational fear of pygmies. Apparently she saw a film once in which some pygmies—"

"Don't," said Roger. "I can imagine. Africa is a vast continent, and there are really very few pygmies about. I, for example, have never seen one. Not that our pygmy population is not quite a distinguished one in its own right. But does Lyonesse have any sense of how Clarice is leaning? In regard to my suit?"

"I gather that Clarice feels that you are the choicest object to canter onto her checkerboard in modern times."

"Hardly the impression she gives me."

"Clarice is a busy and successful woman. Her profession means much to her. If you could knock over a train or something, that might recommend you. Be a commitment, of a kind."

"I really don't feel up to criminality. It would make me most uncomfortable. I'm already uncomfortable as a black in a white world. I'd be doubly so as a professional villain. Why, think you, have I embraced knighthood, when so many other, more intellectually rewarding occupations beckoned? I'll tell you. To make a statement about what one of our revered African leaders, Léopold Senghor, calls *negritude*."

"That's very worshipful of you, Roger, and consonant with that nobility which graces your every gesture. But in this case it doesn't get the job done, does it?"

"There's that."

"Wouldn't have to be a very large train. A local, say from Ipswich to Stowmarket, would do. You could disguise yourself."

"As what? Mr. Bones?"

"I suppose not."

"Besides, I feel a battle coming, a great, epoch-making battle. I must save my strength."

"What have you heard? Is it the invasion?"

"No, worse luck. Mordred is gathering his forces to have it out with Arthur. There are signs everywhere, for those who can read them. Have you noticed the number of priests in the markets? What are they doing? Buying oil for the last rites, that's what—the holy viaticum. The casketmakers toil through the night. Casket-grade pine not to be had anywhere. The farmers are cutting their fields. Better to lay up unripe corn in your barns than have it thrashed to muck by contesting armies."

"I'd best rejoin my unit, then."

"Might be as well."

"What will the outcome be, d'you think?"

"Bitterness. Whichever way goes the day."

IT IS the greatest battle that ever was!"

"Mordred's forces are as many as the leaves of the trees!"

"Arthur's are fewer but braver!"

"So many valorous deeds and noble feats are being done that I have trouble keeping them all in view!"

"A vast canvas, obscured here and there by smoke and flame and dust!"

"Great mischief being hewed on helms and hauberks! Rushing and riding, foining and striking!"

"A grimly clamor as of a thousand anvils being struck!"

"Just counting the breastplates with spears sticking out of them is more than mortal man can do!"

"Yonder knights hurtle together like rams to bear either other down!"

"That one must pull thrice upon his sword to retrieve it from the brainpan of his fallen foe!"

"Now that one has gouged him sorely in the ham!"

"The field encrimsoned with gore of the finest provenance!"

"Launcelot and Sir Roger are shoulder to shoulder in the thickest of the fight!"

"Gawain and Gareth smiting and smiting!"

"Agravain and Algoval dealing many a sad stroke to the teeming multitudes!"

"A few varlets creep about below the battle, robbing the fallen of their purses and jewels!"

"O vilest of the vile! But there, that one has got a poniard in his gut from a knight fallen but not dead!"

"Sir Bedevere has single-handedly taken an entire battery of 105 mm howitzers! The captured gunners line up with their hands behind their heads!"

"O noble Sir Bedevere! Sir Ironside is lashing with his ancient blade as one enchafed by a fiend!"

"But Mordred, too, is doing mighty deeds! He fights extremely well for a traitorous poltroon!"

"He strives with Sir Villiars the Valiant! They rash together like two boars!"

"How can he win these great hosts to his side? For they are as many as the sands of the sea!"

"Some deluded folk feel that Arthur offers only war and strife, but Mordred joy and bliss, and thus flock to Mordred's banner, whether it be right or no!"

"Many a full bold baron is today laid low from wrong thinking and knurled ideas!"

"This horrible carnage must comfort our enemies everywhere!"

"Yes, they must be pleased beyond measure to see our people rashing each other to flinders!"

"What will the outcome of the fracas be?"

"No man can say, except for dole a-plenty!"

LAUNCELOT hanging his great head, sweating and bleeding.

"Jesu," he said. "I'm getting a little old for this."

"Well," said Arthur, "the field is ours, that's the main thing."

"At great cost," said Launcelot. "I counted the dead, just an estimate, of course. They seemed as many as the birds of the air."

"The scavengers have made a pile of the swords of the fallen," said Sir Kay. "It reaches as high as seven refrigerators stacked one atop another."

"Seven stacked refrigerators," said Arthur. "Your figure has a distressing modernity to it."

"Can't be helped. Swords hammered into refrigerators, refrigerators hammered into swords— it's the currency of today."

"Things were quite dicey there for a bit," said Launcelot. "When he threw in his reserves, from behind the hill with the rather ugly church on it, I began to think better of his generalship. It was the right moment."

"Didn't help him much," said Arthur. "Did you see Bedevere come roaring in from the left? A gladsome sight indeed."

"Much people were slain just at that little fork

where the little stream joins the other at the bottom of the hill," said Sir Kay. "Did you see that? Cador of Cornwall was there, with his battle, and they bruised the enemy very prettily. The carnage was like a hundred auto crashes."

"Mordred's traitorous and vile thrust at Arthur went wide, Jesu be praised," said Launcelot. "I saw it. Such maugre cannot be believed."

"He tried," said Arthur. "We were visor to visor. He said, 'The next time,' and then two other knights came between us."

"He got away, with some half-dozen followers, so far as is known," said Sir Kay. "Did you notice he had his dogs with him? I saw one of them clinging to the hindquarters of Gingalin's horse before he was flung off."

"Didn't see it," said Arthur. "Some chap ran at me with a spear and then a mortar round landed right in front of me and blew us both off our feet and then Sir Lucan the Butler came up with a spare horse and then—"

"So the Prophecy was wrong," said Sir Kay, after a bit.

"I don't know that it was wrong," said Arthur. "Perhaps I read it wrongly."

"What's this?" asked Launcelot.

"The sixth part of Merlin's Prophecy appears to suggest that Arthur will die by Mordred's hand in a great battle," said Sir Kay. "This would seem to be it. I daresay there'll never be another on this scale."

"I must confess something," said Arthur. "After I showed it to you I got to thinking about it, the Prophecy, and, well, the short form is, I altered a few lines here and there."

"You *tampered with* Merlin's Prophecy?"

"Yes. I had him predict a slightly more favorable outcome. It's a skill he taught me himself, altering history. Even Caesar used to do it when he read the auguries, you know. He'd diddle the chicken bones, as it were, so that when cast they'd indicate victory for his legions."

"An offense against scholarship, among other things," said Sir Kay.

"All part of kingship," said Arthur. "In a *crise* the king holds nothing sacred—not the past, not the future, and especially not dead mountebanks."

ORDRED has fled to Germany, they say," said Clarice. "He has become a Nazi."

"Always was, by temperament," said Sir Roger.

"And Arthur has annulled the marriage vows which previously bound sweet Lyonesse to that *cochon* Unthank. The marriage is no more. This, incidentally, frees her modest dot, amounting to five freeholds, three small castles, twelve ecclesiastical livings, and a bank, medium-sized bank, for their future enjoyment."

"Very good," said Roger. "Solves the Harrods problem."

"America has entered the war, they say."

"On which side?"

"Ours."

"Splendid," said Roger. "They have no tradition of chivalry, I believe, but they are said to make good soldiers. I need merely instance Stonewall Jackson and Mad Anthony Wayne."

"Names not known to me, but I am delighted, dear friend, to defer to your greater grasp. The Hanged Man has become a warrant officer in the judge advocate general's office."

"Where his talent for logic-chopping will serve him well."

"Haw-Haw is saying that you and I are engaging in miscegenation."

"And so we are. After tea, I hope."

"Possibly even before. Although I'm meant to do a tiny little greengrocer's at two. Should be back at three-thirty at the latest."

"Does this involve risk to yourself? Whom I love above all other beings?"

"Only in theory. Teddy is driving and Tommy will do the wire-cutting, so I feel perfectly safe."

"Still—"

"You were amazing in the great battle," said Clarice. "You were as one enchafed by a fiend."

"Well, we won, that's the main thing. But it was the last battle of its kind, I feel. There will be other Mordreds, but Arthur will never countenance another fratricidal war. And he won't manufacture the bomb, but someone else is certain to, and then we'll have the hellish thing with us for eternity. Be like having a volcano in the parlor."

"Not much call for your particular skills in such a world," she said. "All you good and worshipful knights out of work. On the dole. Not a pretty picture."

"I have another string or two to my lute," said Roger. "My degrees are in engineering, biochemistry, canon law, archaeology, and marine architecture."

"Quite a handy fellow, aren't you? Ever been a wheelman?"

"It's Launcelot I worry about," Roger said. "There are figures of such magnificence, such legendary proportions, that they're . . . encumbered, as it were. Ordinary life is not possible, in such a case. Can you see Launcelot running a small factory somewhere? Or even a large factory? I fear psychic disintegration."

"And Guinevere," said Clarice. "What of Guinevere?"

"Fixed in sorrow and longing," said Roger. "Forever a paradigm of the divided heart."

"But managing to have a suspiciously good time along the way."

"The ground theme is the divided heart. I did a paper on the phenomenon once, for a course I had in passion."

"You had to be taught passion?"

"A general study of the passions, with special attention to their biochemical triggers."

"You mean it's all just sort of Pavlovian?"

"No no. It's very specialized. Hardly a woman in a thousand causes the appropriate neurons to fire."

"That many."

"Sometimes it's just orange blossoms, with no woman attached, isn't it? You must remember that men are very delicate, very suggestible. Memory and desire, as that bank poet put it."

"To work," said Clarice. "Heigh-ho."

"I think I'll take a nap," said Sir Roger. "Try not to shoot anyone, there's a dear girl."

IR BREUNOR le Noire has disappeared! He's not to be found anywhere! I went to his quarters to seek him, but they were empty! He's neither in the stables nor on the exercise field!"

"Perhaps he's out adventuring!"

"His horses are here!"

"I cannot lay hand to Sir Grummor Grummorson! I had a message for him from Sir Kay, and sought to deliver it, and searched for him high and low, and he was nowhere to be seen!"

"Sir Harry le Fise Lake, that was a Templar, is gone too! I looked for him in chapel—he spends hours at his devotions—but he was not there, nor was he seeing to his 'quipage nor having him a meal nor in the necessary house!"

"Certes, it is an odd business! Duke Eustace of Canbenet is gone from his lands, so they say, and so are Hermance, King of the Orange City, and Brastias of Tintagel!"

"It is as if there were a mighty conclave at some place we know not of! Dornard, son of Pellinor, has vanished, and so, too, Alisander l'Orphelin!"

"Berrrant l'Apres is gone, and with him his hundred knights! Also Tor le Fise de Vayshoure, Urre of the Mount, and Nentres, King of Garlot!"

"Uwain le Blanchemains is not at his castle, nor

Sir Perimones, Sir Kehydius, Sir Lucan the Butler, Sir Brian of the Isles, Sir Galagars, Sir Helin le Blank, Sir Meliagaunt, nor Sir Ozana le Cure Hardy!"

"Gone, flown, disappeared! King Leodegrance of Camelerd is absent a fortnight, and the kingdom languishes without him! Florence, Gawain's son, is fled or spirited away, no one knows, and Sir Gingalin with him, and Idrus, son of Unwain, and Accolon of Gaul, and Bellengerus le Beuse!"

"It is as if all of chivalry has gathered itself in some remote place, far from here, that is known only to those who are in it!"

"Gone, flown, disappeared! King Carados of Scotland, Sir Gilbert the Bastard, Sir Meliot de Logris, Sir Ulfius, Lavaine the son of Bernard of Astolat, King Rience of North Wales, King Howel of Brittany, King Lot of Lothian . . ."

T IS so fine and pleasant to go a-Maying, in the daffodil time, with apple blossoms, cherry blossoms—"

"Your majesty."

"Yes."

" 'Tis no longer May."

"What's that you say?"

" 'Tis May no longer. This is November."

"November. Methought I felt a chill upon the air."

"And that you did."

"A chill upon the air, and the meadow grasses gone to dun, and wrinkling brown things depending from the vines—"

"And the bombs blowing up everything, mum, and the great fires, and the people without houses, and the dead people with their arms blown off, or their legs or their heads—"

"I thought I was a-Maying still."

"You've been too much time in the hospitals, my lady; it's affected your mind."

"No, I'm merely a bit tired, Varley. What time is it?"

"The clocks have stopped, all of them. I'll turn on the radio, mum."

147

"Don't. It'll be either the one villain babbling about the Jews or the other villain telling us that the U-boats have got one of our convoys."

"Sir Robert is here."

"I don't want to see him. I know what he's here to say."

"He's been waiting for hours."

"Send him away. I have the vapors, I think, or perhaps the mopes, and for all I know it is communicable, and I would not wish that splendid knight and stalwart defender of the realm Sir Robert to be subjected to inconvenience of that sort merely on my account—"

"Yes, send him away," said Sir Robert, entering, "throw the bloody man out and give him a kick in the crutch on the stairs—"

"But, good Sir Robert, surely you have come to say that which I most do not wish to hear. Wherefore should I hear it, then? Get you gone and make no speeches."

"It is farewell, but it is only temporary. I hope."

"You are a ruffian just like all the other ruffians, like Arthur, like Launcelot, here today and gone tomorrow, constancy not in you, nor the gift of hope to give me—"

"There is a reason. What I am doing is what all of chivalry is doing, every knight and squire that walks the earth, all of the same mind and purpose—"

"Reason me no reasons, 'tis not a reasoning matter, it is a matter of the heart, and if you had one, rather than a tin of biscuits, in your manly Scots chest, you would—"

Then Guinevere swooned, and Sir Robert swooned, and Varley, seeing them swooned, swooned away too.

FTER the battle," said Launcelot, "I was riding alone, and I chanced upon a great house that had been fled by its inhabitants. But looters had been there, and everywhere on the grounds there was evidence of their diligence. There were bits of tables and chairs of fine mahogany lying on the grass, and also large shards of silk paper that had been torn from the interior walls. Pieces of broken mirror mingled with fragments of costly brocades, window coverings, and hundreds of glass lights from several chandeliers, the skeletons of which lay in a heap in a courtyard. Broken marble, broken Sèvres in the grass, and ripped-apart cushions, and wounded and burnt mattresses, and parts of a piano, and portraits that had been shot at as if they were targets in a shooting gallery."

"Ugly," Guinevere said.

"There was the corpse of a dog, an Irish setter, dark red blood on the red mahogany coat, and a parcel-gilt frame, robbed of its picture and cracked in two pieces, had been flung about it. The very trees had been hacked, drunkenly I suppose, and the lawns trampled by many horses, and the sides of the house were scorched where fires had been built against them, and books in the embers, and things were written on the walls, ungodlinesses of every kind. Bits of brass fixtures torn from the bathrooms, broken kitchen knives, the clothes belonging to the owners had all been carried off save, here and there, a stray stocking or ripped pair of trousers or a smashed hat.

"I was constrained to dismount and pick up a book, a token of the library pillaged there. The first one I looked at was printed in a language I did not know and contained chess diagrams."

"And now you're going away."

"Yes."

"You're always and forever going away. Nothing new there."

"No."

"No words honeyed or other can stay you. Even the myth-creating queen cannot stay you."

"You've been talking to Lyonesse."

"We are like the bee, queens. I mean the queen bee. The world revolves around us. The world except for you. You are as beclosed in iron. You don't revolve."

"I am seemly and demure as the dove."

"The next myth I create will be a hellacious one, of that you may be sure. Something so wicked I can't even imagine it now. I'll have to give it study."

"I'll read about it. In *News of the World*."

"Something truly horrible, in very good taste, of course. Screaming headlines. You'll be proud of me."

"As ever, dear queen."

"Go then. Before I get upset."

"I am gone."

HE ROOF is leaking," said Guinevere, "although I don't suppose you care."

"I have never yet owned a castle where the roof did not leak at one point or another," said Arthur. "The entelechy of roofs is to leak, something the architect Griegsmore taught me long, long ago. Why, madam, may I ask, are you favoring me with this information? Have we no staff in this blasted place?"

Guinevere straddling Arthur's right leg, tugging on the right boot. Arthur's left foot planted at her spine's base.

"I tell you not because I expect you to do anything about it," said Guinevere, "but because you are my husband and it is the sort of thing one tells a husband if one has a husband nearby. I mean the sort of thing that most wives would tell most husbands if the husband was within shouting distance. Most husbands pay attention to things of this sort, if only momentarily, on the fly, as it were, notational as it were between very much more important matters—"

"Your imitation of humility is quite the worst I have ever encountered," Arthur said. "I suspect the films. Have you been going to the films?"

"I see one now and again," said Guinevere. "It fills the time."

"I saw one years and years ago. It was quite exciting. It was about a train robbery. These fellows climbed aboard a train and robbed it. They had handkerchiefs over their faces so that no one could identify them. Then they got back on their horses and rode away. Most satisfying."

"I put a pot under it," she said, "or rather, several pots, because it's a cluster of leaks, rather than a —"

"Haw-Haw has been saying that you've been sleeping with a certain Brown Knight," said Arthur. "A Scot, I gather. Any truth in it?"

"There was someone," Guinevere said, "recently, within the last fortnight, a Scot? I don't think so, they speak in a strange manner, do they not? from rather deep in the throat, this fellow was not like that, as I recall, a slender lad, hardly a knight I should think, no scars on him, lovely long legs, lovely long thin slightly curved—"

"Why do I always have the feeling that what you are telling me is true in essence if not necessarily in detail?"

"It is trust," said Guinevere, "the trust which has always endured between us and has ennobled our union from start to finish."

"From start to finish?"

"Just an expression," said Guinevere. "How was your trip?"

"Well, it was one damn thing after another," said Arthur. "I suppose you've heard we lost Tobruk. Again."

"I did."

"Wasn't supposed to happen. I flew out there to try to buck up the theatre commander. It was as if I wasn't there. Chap said all the right things, mind, steadfast resolve, waiting for the psychological moment, the bold stroke, all that. Then he let Rommel roll up his left flank like wallpaper. Damnedest thing I ever saw."

"Winston's man, I suppose."

"Of course. But I could have chosen him, just as well. I can't blame Winston. One never knows until after the fact how these fellows will perform. With *our* people, one knows."

"Still," said Guinevere, "I like the idea of there being new players on the board. It makes things more interesting, don't you think."

"This is not a game. It is a war and one we may very well lose. And I've done something rather awful."

"What?"

"I've surrendered an advantage. A wonderful advantage, or would have been, to our side. I said no. Because I thought it immoral."

"I'm sure you did the right thing. You *always* do the right thing."

"Are you being critical? Is that a criticism?"

"Not at all. So we'll go to the mountains. Resist from the mountains."

"Perhaps not literally. But in a way, yes."

"I'm ready," she said.

"You and I and our kind can go to the mountains," Arthur said. "Most of the world can't."

"I know," said Guinevere. "Children in school, dental problems, old aunties hanging by a thread, books to be written, the lottery, flirtations, winter wheat—"

"Precisely," said the king. "Your grasp of the total situation remains, as ever, excellent."

"*Merde,*" said Guinevere. "What queens are for. But you, dear Arthur, are a bit at sixes and sevens, in terms of legend. You require, legend requires, a tragic end."

"It will find me, never fear," said the king. "No particular hurry, I suppose?"

"I can wait," said the queen.

"IR LAUNCELOT lieth under an apple tree, sleeping!"

"Why is he not riding, ceaselessly riding, from one adventure to the next?"

"Perhaps he is fatigued!"

"Every time he lieth under an apple tree, sleeping, some enchantress draws near and casts a spell upon him and tries to get him into her bed by tricherie!"

"Look you, even now there comes one who is clearly an enchantress! She hath the visage of an enchantress, the hair of an enchantress, the garb of an enchantress, and the hat of an enchantress!"

"Who are those people with her?"

"Those are fifty giants which had been engendered of fiends, such as one normally finds in the entourage of an enchantress!"

"She is holding a mantle, the richest mantle that ever was seen, as full of precious stones as the night of fireflies! Doubtless she will lay it upon Launcelot, that he not be taken with the ague!"

"An' she were to lay it upon him, he is a dead man, for it is the type of mantle that, when you are wrapped in it, you are burnt to a clinker!"

"The sorceress is none other than Margot de L'Eaux Distraits, who witched Sir Bors and Sir Bedevere and made them paramours to sheep!"

"That were hanging about their loved sheep, and mooning, and striking the harp for the sheep, and indulging in all manner of unchaste behaviors, and got the bloat in their testicles and must take to their beds for many months!"

"But now Launcelot stirs in his sleep. He lifts an arm and the arm throws the wretched mantle onto a giant, who burns to a frizzle!"

"Sweet Jesu, the smell! Yon burning giant smells like a tavern mattress!"

"All the other giants flee, and with them Margot, lest Launcelot come fully awake and wax wroth!"

"But Launcelot sleeps on, undisturbed! I wonder what he's dreaming."

"He is dreaming that there is no war, no Table Round, no Arthur, no Launcelot!"

"That cannot be! He dreams, rather, of the softness of Guinevere, the sweetness of Guinevere, the brightness of Guinevere, and the sexuality of Guinevere!"

"How do you know?"

"I can see into the dream! Now she enters the dream in her own person, wearing a gown wrought of gold bezants over white samite and carrying a bottle of fine wine, Pinot Grigio by the look of it!"

"What a matchless dream!"

"Under an apple tree . . ."

THE KING
was completed by Donald Barthelme
in May 1989.
The book was set in Galliard
with fifteenth-century ornamental initials
from the *Summa Bartholomaei Pisani*.
The design and original wood engravings
are by Barry Moser.

SELECTED DALKEY ARCHIVE PAPERBACKS

FOR A FULL LIST OF PUBLICATIONS, VISIT:

www.dalkeyarchive.com

SELECTED DALKEY ARCHIVE PAPERBACKS

FOR A FULL LIST OF PUBLICATIONS, VISIT:
www.dalkeyarchive.com